MW00655012

Crying on Airplanes

A novel by

Lo Palomar

Copyright © 2021 LOProductions
San Diego, CA

All rights reserved.

No part of this book may be reproduced in any form or by
any electronic or mechanical means, including information
storage and retrieval systems, without written permission
from the publisher or author, except in the case of
a reviewer, who may quote brief passages embodied in
critical articles or in a review.

Crying on Airplanes is a work of fiction. The circumstances
and characters in the book are purely fictional. Any
similarities between them and real individuals living, or
dead are purely coincidental. Some Dallas, Texas and
Mexico City establishments are mentioned, but are again
used fictitiously.

Cover Art Design by Chris Marroy

Key Contributor: Erin Shaw

Edited by Leah Campbell and Erin Shaw

ISBN 978-0-578-91747-4

To Austen, Morgan, and Rebecca, this book would not exist without you. Thank you for the inspiration, encouragement, and laughter always. I will forever be thankful for your friendship and our group text.

To my Mexico City team, thank you for believing in me, coaching me, and for exploring your beautiful city with me. I will always look back on our project fondly.

PROLOGUE

One Week Ago

"What did he just say?" Charles asked me in a panicked tone. "Did he say a head?!"

Wide eyed, I heard Jake say it again, "Es una cabeza..."

I couldn't believe what I was hearing and looked back at Charles. He looked pale and terrified. When I finally found the words, I responded, "Yes."

The package sat on the floor, dark blood oozing out of the bottom of it.

"Oh, hell no," Max caught a glimpse of the box and couldn't get away fast enough. He ducked into the bathroom, and we all heard him retching.

I looked at Jake. "¿Qué piensas? Who do you think it is?"

"I'm not sure." He seemed stunned, so I took the lead.

"Jake, call security."

"Huh?" he wasn't listening.

"Call security!" I said again. "Everyone else, into the conference room. Now."

I led everyone back into the conference room, trying to decipher what to do next. I heard Jake on the phone to security team and the words that came out of his mouth were surreal.

"Si, hay una cabeza en la caja. No, no se de quien." He didn't know whose head it is. He hadn't wanted to touch it because he knew it would be tampering with evidence of a crime. It could be someone we knew. "Por favor apúrate." He begged them to hurry.

This is exactly what everyone told me would happen if I came to Mexico City. Still, I couldn't believe their nightmare had become my reality—I could hardly process it.

I sat down and tried to compose myself, placing my head in my hands. I muttered to myself, "I didn't want them to be right." A severed head in a box, mailed to our office. It was so horrifyingly cliché.

I had fallen in love with Mexico City. I loved the work we were doing; I loved the people I had met, and then... there was Gio.

The instant I thought of him, I realized that I still hadn't heard back from him.

Frantic, I grabbed my phone. I dialed his number, and it went straight to voicemail. "Gio, where are you?! Call me! Please!"

CHAPTER ONE
The Opportunity

Six Months Ago

You know those moments where it feels like the universe is conspiring to change something in your life? It's like one moment you're just sitting there, drinking coffee, and nibbling on toast when all of a sudden everything changes. For me it happened when I was home in San Diego, California for the holidays. I was sitting at my parent's kitchen table, reading the news over breakfast. The rays of the morning sun beamed in through the sheer kitchen curtains. It was the first that I'd been home since I started my new job with Global Core Consulting—my very first, post-collegiate, grown-up job. I was finishing my second piece of toast when I saw the headline in the paper, PacificSouth to Acquire Timbre from Grupo Merced in record time to expand their presence south of the border.

"Oh!" I said aloud without meaning to. I hadn't realized that this was happening. I continued reading. PacSouth was my client, and they were about to acquire Grupo Merced's telecommunications division in Mexico City. I started to get excited. I had told my boss Jake when I interviewed for the job that speaking Spanish in a business setting was my dream. All those years of studying Spanish would finally have a purpose. I paused and thought for a moment. Was it too forward to express interest in working on this deal? A wry smile started to pull at my cheek, and I decided to take a chance. I pulled out my phone and started typing.

Hi Jake –

I saw the news about the PacificSouth and Timbre acquisition. Not sure if we are going to support them on the integration activities but I would appreciate the opportunity to support you on the proposal, if so.

I hope you are enjoying the holidays.

Best,

Blake

I reread the note a few times before hitting send. Finally, I pressed the button and heard the sound effect as my email whooshed through the air toward Jake's inbox. I took a deep breath and exhaled.

It felt like I'd barely finished expelling my breath when my phone started to buzz, and Jake's name popped up on the screen. It was either good news, or I'd crossed a line. I gulped audibly as I picked up the call.

"Hi Jake," I said, trying to sound casual.

"Blake, it's Jake." Being the no-nonsense guy that he was, he got straight to the point. "Listen, we are working on a proposal to support PacificSouth and I could use some help. We had a team member who was working with us on it, but she's bowed out because she doesn't speak Spanish. Are you willing to lean in over the holidays?"

I felt my heart lift. "Yes! Of course!" I answered without thinking about my family's holiday plans. Oh well, I thought. This was a once in a lifetime career opportunity and I was not going to let it pass.

"Great," Jake said. "I'll send you some of the official deal documents. I need you to read through them and synthesize the key points. We can discuss tomorrow."

"Okay! I can do that."

"Thank you."

"Of course!"

"Oh, and Blake," he said. "You know that if we win this work, you may have the opportunity to work in Mexico, so start thinking about if that is something you would like to do."

I had to stop myself from blurting out, "Duh!" into the phone. Before I could respond at all he said, "Talk tomorrow." And hung up the call. I heard a ding on my phone and opened my email. I had already received all of the deal docs from Jake and couldn't help but shake my head at the speed with which he moved. There were two legal documents making up more than 200 pages to read. I had a momentary feeling of regret that I might have bitten off more than I could chew, but I tried to push past my feelings.

"Blake, honey..." My mom entered my room, "It's time to go." I stared up at her like a deer in the headlights. "Lunch! At Hotel Del with the family. Remember?"

I looked down at the toast on my plate and then back up at her. "Mom... I'm so sorry. I'm not going to be able to make it."

"Why not?" She looked surprised.

"Our client just acquired a company in Mexico, and I just received hundreds of pages of legal documents that I need to read by tomorrow."

She gave me a look like that just wouldn't do. "Blake, it's the holidays." She cocked her head at me thoughtfully, but I could tell she was disappointed. "I thought you were taking time off?"

"You and me both," I joked.

"I don't see how this is funny. We rarely get to see you as it is."

"I know, Mom... but I'm the new girl at the firm, and I'm lowest on the totem pole. I feel like I'm not in a position to say no to my boss right now." I wasn't about to tell her that I'd basically asked for the extra work.

"Well, alright." She conceded. "I'll let your dad know." She started to walk out of the kitchen.

"Thank you," I called after her. "I really appreciate it! It's a great opportunity for me! Plus, this project could give me the opportunity to work in Mexico City, which would be amaz—"

"Mexico?" She stopped dead in her tracks and then walked back into the room to face me.

"Wouldn't that be amazing!?" I couldn't contain my excitement at the thought. "I could actually use my Spanish degree in a business setting. That's the dream!"

"Blake..." She hesitated. "Let's just talk about all of this later, okay?" She walked out of the room again.

"Okay," I said, opening my computer.

"And try to get everything done today so we can enjoy tomorrow!"

"Will do!" I clicked open the first document and started reading.

The next day was Christmas Eve and I had gotten all of the requested materials to Jake. He seemed pleased with the output and suggested I enjoy the next few days before we were back in the office. "We're back on the 27th and things are going to move fast," he'd said.

As my family trickled in for dinner, champagne was popped, and appetizers were enjoyed. My relatives were eager to hear about my new job and my grandpa started the questioning.

"So, what's it like being a working girl?" he asked me.

"It's great!" I said, as I finished chewing the last bit of jalapeno popper. "Although it has been an adjustment. I'm getting up every morning at 6:00AM to get to the office by 7:00AM, I'm learning new business jargon and paying all my own bills for the first time in my life."

"One off the payroll!" my dad cheerfully chimed in and clanked his wine glass against my mom's champagne glass.

"Well, good for you Blake. What are you working on, anything interesting?" My grandpa continued.

"Actually..." I started to smile. "I'm working on a confidential merger right now, which I can't tell you about."

My grandpa smiled at me conspiratorially and then nodded in agreement. "I gotcha," he said. All those years of working for the government were still deeply ingrained in him.

"I can tell you that my client just acquired another business in Mexico City, and I am hoping I can transition to working on that project."

"Mexico?!" My grandma Mary Jo almost spit out her champagne and then looked at my dad. "John? She can't be serious!"

"What?" My dad looked confused.

"Mexico is not safe," my grandma scolded. "My neighbor's daughter's friend went missing when they were on spring break in college, and they later found her body in the back of a taxi with all of her organs missing."

"Jo!" My grandpa looked shocked.

"Mom, stop with the horror stories," my dad said. "We're getting ahead of ourselves. Blake isn't even sure if she's going yet. And hypothetically if Blake goes to Mexico City, it'll be for work. Companies have security." My dad seemed pretty blasé about the situation, but my mom looked concerned.

Grandma Mary Jo huffed at my dad and turned to me. "Blake, it is not safe there. You really shouldn't go."

"We'll just see what happens, grandma," I said.

Back in Dallas the proposal did indeed move quickly. Jake had been true to his word. Given the speed with which the deal had closed, the PacificSouth team needed help ASAP. Jake came into the bullpen where all of the analysts and consultants on our team sat. It was a dimly lit office space in the basement of our client's offices.

"¿Blake, donde aprendist Español?" He pulled up a chair close to where I was working and sat down by straddling the back of the chair. He wanted to know where I learned Spanish.

The other analyst and consultants in the room looked up from their computers and stared at me, "Aprendi en la Universidad y estudi en España dos veces diferente," I answered.

My colleague Maxwell, or Max as he liked to be called, looked at me wide eyed. "What did you say?" he asked, perplexed.

"She said she learned it in college and studied in Spain twice," Jake answered. "¿Y cuantos años has hablado Español?"

"Probablemente quience anos. That's fifteen years," I said, turning to Max. Jake and I continued back and forth, in Spanish and Max just laughed.

"Y'all are going to have to translate for me when we get there," he said, turning back to his computer.

"Is that really happening?" I asked, excitedly. "Seriously!?"

"Seriously. Assuming you still want to come. Max, Charles y George no hablan Español y van a necistar ayuda." Jake smiled and stood up. I was shaking my head vigorously yes. "We fly out on Sunday night—book your flight."

"You didn't know you were coming?" Max asked.

"No!" I exclaimed.

"Well, you're ready," he said. "Mexico! It's gonna be... calliente, I think... is that the word?"

Max was a more senior strategy consultant who had joined Global Core after business school. He had been with the firm for a few years and had made a point over the last few months to train me on all things consulting. He had developed a list of Jake and George's pet peeves, our leads on our current project, he taught me all of the Powerpoint and Excel shortcuts I needed to know and helped me with some of our clients' most absurd asks. I would have been lost without his help.

I opened up a browser window on my computer to book my flight and just then, George walked by. "Blake, I hear you will be joining us in Mexico City?"

"Yeah!" I answered.

"Excited I see! Well, get lots of rest we're looking at long hours in a foreign city."

"I can't wait," I smiled.

"Well, I love the enthusiasm."

As we inched closer and closer to leaving for Mexico City, I found that my enthusiasm remained steadfast, but it began to co-mingle with other feelings like nervousness. The scope of the project and the trip began to weigh on me a bit. I had never been away from my home country this long and the stakes for this project were very high. Several days in a row I started to pack only to get overwhelmed and find other things I needed to do instead. After cleaning my apartment top to bottom, re-organizing my spice cabinet, and cleaning my baseboards, I decided I couldn't avoid it any longer, so I called in reinforcements.

"Okay girl, let's get you packed! Wow, it's so clean in here!" My best friend Mia arrived with a bottle of wine to help me accomplish the task at hand. Mia was my best friend at SMU and was pretty much the main reason why I stayed in Dallas after graduating. She was my chosen family and the idea of moving away from her was impossible. As I saw her face, it hit me how long I was really going to be away, and I started to feel the slightest bit emotional.

"I'm so glad you're here!" I pulled her into a tight hug and blinked the beginnings of tears away.

As Mia found glasses and the wine opener in the kitchen, I pulled out my biggest suitcase and started pulling my work clothes out of my closet and arranging them on my bed.

Mia returned with a glass of wine and stared at the pile. "What is all of that?" she asked, sounding scandalized.

"My work clothes..."

"Okay, sister, you're going to Mexíco!" she said, pronouncing the country's name the way you do in Spanish. She handed me a glass and she clinked hers to mine. "You have to have a few fun things too!" She went to my closet and pulled out the bright red dress that I had worn on my 21st birthday in Las Vegas. "Throw this in your bag just in case?"

"Mia! I don't think I'll be needing a club dress. I'll be working!"

"You never know who you might meet! It's been six months since you and Scott split. What if you find a hot Latin lover who fills you with passión!" She gave me a little wink and shimmied her shoulders in front of the dress.

"Doubtful!" I replied. "I'll be working, remember? Voy a trabajar. ¿Recuerda?"

"Fine, well let's at least pack you a few cute tops and jeans."

"Okay okay—" My phone pinged, and I looked down. I had an email from work with the subject line: Travel Warning.

"B? Everything okay?" Mia asked.

"Yeah..." I started to read the email.

WARNING: An itinerary you have upcoming is for a country or city that has travel restrictions and guidelines: Do not travel alone; stay with your team.

Stay at one of the pre-approved hotels.

Do not take taxis; Only take cars set up previously through Global Core Consulting. If you have any issues, please contact this number (888) 555-3426 and head immediately to your country's specific embassy. Your safety is our top priority. If at any point you feel unsafe, please consult our team about return travel home.

"Jesus," I whispered under my breath.

"What is it?" Mia asked.

"Global Core just sent an email about all the safety precautions we should take while in Mexico City. Maybe Mexico City isn't as safe as I thought..."

I looked up at her and she had a bit of a concerned look on her face. She walked over and put her arm around me. "Blake, I really think you'll be fine. Just be smart, and maybe don't take a Latin lover unless he's been vetted by your work friends."

I laughed. "Right."

"You've got this, girl."

I nodded at her, and we hugged. "I'm really going to miss you while I'm gone," I said, my eyes welling up again.

"I know, but we'll FaceTime all the time. And you better text me photos every single time you have Wifi!"

"I will."

We finished the wine; we finished the packing, and I zipped my bag up and left it near my front door. Once Mia left, I made sure my car service was scheduled for the morning and I double checked to make sure I was all checked in for my flight. As I climbed into bed that night, I took a deep breath and steadied myself. Everything was going to be fine. It was time to get to work.

CHAPTER TWO

La Aventura

"You're calling to try and talk me out of going, aren't you?" I answered the phone with a question. It was rare that Grandma Mary Jo called me on a Sunday. She reserved that day for attending church and having lunch with the priest. So, when I saw she was calling me, I knew it must be about my trip.

"Really Blake, aren't there other places you could go for work? You know bad things happen in Mexico. What if you get kidnapped, or worse?"

"Grandma, we already talked about this. It's a work trip. I'm going with my entire team. I speak Spanish and so do several others. We are going to be meeting colleagues there who are locals. It'll be okay, I promise."

"Well, you're worrying me, you know and it's not great for my blood pressure."

"I know..." I said. "But I'll be checking in with my parents regularly and they said they'll update you on all of my adventures."

This kind of call had been a regular occurrence over the last few weeks. My grandma wasn't used to not getting her way and I could tell she was disappointed that I was still going. My parents and my brothers were all supportive but had become increasingly nervous. They wanted me to check in with them as often as possible.

And then there was Scott. We had decided to take some space after graduation, and we hadn't talked very often since that time. I think he had it in his mind that we might give it another try eventually and when he heard that I was going to Mexico City, he had called to tell me that it was definitely over.

"I'm really surprised you're making this choice, Blake," he'd said. "You're really making it difficult for us to truly know if we're right for each other."

"Well, I think some distance may help," I'd told him.

Sure, it was a big deal heading to Mexico City for almost a year to work on a high-profile multi-billion-dollar M&A deal, but I was ready. This was why I wanted to pursue a career in consulting. I was excited about the new project; I trusted my team and I trusted myself. I was street smart, had good instincts and was ready for an adventure. Since Jake had given me the green light, I'd spent every waking minute reading up on Mexico City. I wanted to learn all about the neighborhoods, the great places to visit and eat. I had nearly memorized the metro map. I felt prepared. I spoke Spanish fluently. What could possibly go wrong?

I sighed. "Grandma, I'm twenty-two. I'm an adult. I need to be able to make decisions for myself. Don't you want that?"

"No."

I laughed. "You know I'm at the airport right now, right?"

"Your grandfather calls it a Hail Mary, honey."

"I love you, Grandma. I'll email you all as soon as I land."

I hung up the call and took a sip of my coffee and glanced at my watch. Our flight was departing in just over an hour. On my right, in the Hudson Newsstand, I saw Max and Charles browsing through books and magazines, talking animatedly. Everyone was excited, and a little nervous too. George was sitting in a chair right next to the gate, his foot tapping busily as he read through paperwork. I could tell he was nervous—he hated flying, which made consulting an interesting career choice. However, he was also in a silent competition with Jake for the next Managing Director position within our team. So, he was doing everything he could to be prepared before we were even wheels up.

Boarding the plane, I felt my own travel jitters revving up. I kept mentally running over the lists of everything I had brought and packed. My passport? Check. Laptop? Check. iPad? My headphones? Check. Check. I couldn't believe I was on my way.

"¡Hola! Bievenidos," the flight attendant welcomed me aboard.

Flying AeroMexico, the second I walked onto the plane I already felt as if I had left the United States. "Buenas Dias," I replied. I walked up the aisle toward my seat and admired how many people were dressed in suits and business attire. It made me feel a little bit under-dressed in my yoga pants and hoodie. As I glanced at the faces, I could have sworn some of them looked like the clients we'd be meeting with at PacificSouth and my stomach was immediately filled with nerves that they'd spot me looking unprofessional.

I found my seat and prepared my iPad and my headphones for the flight. I had the window seat and wasn't anywhere near my colleagues. I took a deep breath and closed my eyes. It felt like the last bit of alone time before we'd be flung into the intensities of the deal.

As the plane began to taxi, I felt such a mixture of emotions that I wasn't sure if I wanted to laugh or cry. It was like my heart was expanding and I could tell in that moment that the next time I touched down at DFW I wouldn't be the same person I was today. It felt like the first great adventure of my adult life.

The flight was unremarkable—a few bumps as we flew over the Gulf, but mostly it was just two-and-a-half hours of the dull hum of the jet engine. I sipped on a ginger ale to ease my nervous stomach and looked through the project onboarding deck. I wanted to learn the names and faces of the major players. As I looked through it, I couldn't help but try to hide my computer screen on the tiny tray table, just in case any of our clients were on the same flight and might see me looking at their bios. My eagerness to begin a project often left me feeling a little anxious at the get go, but this was different. I had put a lot on the line when I'd lobbied Charles and Jake for this project, and I was desperate to prove myself.

Consulting wasn't a career path I ever thought I'd get into. When I was a little girl, I always wanted to be a teacher, and then a sportscaster—right around the time I went to baseball camp with my brother and cousins, but never a specialist in mergers and acquisitions. This line of work was something I fell into by accident, but it invigorated me. I loved the attention to detail, the problem solving, the client interactions, the most senior discussions I had the opportunity to be a part of at twenty-two years old. I was such a fan of organization and most people in consulting were type A, so it was nice to be around like-minded people. I loved the rush of the meetings and it felt good when the deal was closed, wrapped up neatly and tied with a bow.

I was eager to begin this deal. The integration would be a lengthy and complicated process that would require weeks of meetings, budget negotiations, and contractual agreements that would hopefully leave both companies satisfied and my team feeling victorious. Still, there was a lot of work ahead of us.

I leaned my head back and took another sip of my ginger ale and a deep breath. The air flowing out of the vent above my seat cooled my forehead and I willed my excited heartbeat to steady.

Upon landing, I felt a bit calmer. As soon as the wheels touched down and the pilot hit the brakes a smile swept across my face. We had arrived. I watched the other passengers stand up in unison as soon as the fasten seatbelt sign turned off. We filed out of the plane dutifully and headed toward baggage claim. The other members of my team fell in step with me as we walked with purpose to get our bags and head to the hotel.

"I can't believe we're here!" said Max enthusiastically. "Mexico City has been on my list for years!"

"I can't wait to try the food," Charles chimed in.

"You okay, George?" I asked. He was still looking a little pale.

"Just glad we're on the ground," he replied.

"This way, guys," Jake said, pointing us to the baggage carousel area.

Everyone was chatting anxiously as we stood in the customs line. It was jarring to see Mexican federales with large guns in the airport, but also kind of exciting to be in an environment so different from my normal day-to-day life. When it was my turn, I handed my customs form to the officer and smiled. I felt like I needed to give off a positive first impression.

"How long do you plan to be in Mexico City?" he asked me.

"About a year," I replied. "I'm here for work," I added as he eyed me curiously.

"For your work," he said. "What kind of work?"

"I work for Global Core Consulting and we're trying to secure a merger between a US and Mexican company."

His expression suddenly changed, and he looked both surprised and oddly acquiescent. "You can go. Enjoy your time."

"Gracias," I said. *Well, that was easy...*

Once outside, we piled into our cars and headed into town. It was evening and the light in the winter sky was already beginning to darken. The city sparkled as we drove through it. I looked out the window, trying to take everything in. I wanted to memorize the city instantly, eager to claim a piece of it as my own. It didn't matter that I'd only been here about an hour.

Pulling up to the W Hotel, it was impossible not to admire the property. The first three floors were paned entirely in glass, and the lights coming from inside the hotel were vibrant and colorful. I got out of the car and thanked the driver as he handed me my bags. The music coming from inside the hotel immediately captured my attention. All around us, the air was humid even though it was January. It felt thick and tangible that I had the impulse to bat it away from my face.

Max hopped out next and retrieved his own suitcase from the trunk. We thanked the driver again before heading toward the entrance. The second Uber containing Jake, George and Charles pulled up right after ours had pulled away from the curb. We waved to them and stood at the curb waiting for them to get their luggage.

"Wow. Can you believe this?" Max asked, gazing up at the building.

"It's gorgeous," I agreed.

As the rest of the team approached Charles went right into leadership mode. "Let's check in and then maybe meet for dinner in an hour?" he said.

We all agreed. I realized I was starving as we approached the desk to check in. The smells coming from the restaurant in the lobby were intoxicating and I felt my stomach rumble. I hadn't eaten since breakfast. Now that we were here, I was ready to settle in and celebrate a little.

I felt independent standing at the desk, checking in. Everyone behind the concierge desk was dressed pristinely and they were super friendly.

"Here you are ma'am," she said. "We've upgraded you to a suite."

"What?" I was stunned. "That's amazing. Thank you!"

"¡Si! Yes, Of course," she replied. "Welcome."

"Wow! ¡Muchas gracias!" I was a bit stunned as she handed me the key. I glanced over at the rest of the team as they were checking in with other concierge members. They didn't seem fazed by the upgrades, being more seasoned travelers and loyal Bonvoy members. I knew we were going to have nice accommodations, but a suite was not something I was expecting. Max looked at me with a smile. I returned a baffled expression and he laughed.

"You'll get used to it," he said. "I'll teach you all the consulting travel tricks. Don't worry."

I rode the elevator up with my team and then we went to our separate rooms to clean up before dinner. A bit anxious, I pushed the room key into the card reader and stepped into my new temporary home.

My breath caught in my chest as I walked into the suite and then my jaw hit the floor as I took it all in. The room was exquisitely decorated, and it had two levels. It was like a small apartment. The first floor had a small kitchen and living room with a couch and flat screen TV. Then there was a staircase with translucent stairs that led up to the king size sleeping loft.

"Oh my god," I mumbled to myself as I walked around the room, my fingers examining all the textures. Everything was brightly colored, and the furnishings were all hyper-modern. This had to be one of the nicest hotel rooms I had ever stayed in, especially by myself. I instinctively grabbed my phone out of my bag to snap photos to preserve the memories, as if I wouldn't see this view every day for the next several months.

I texted the photos to my parents, and to my best friend Mia. "Still think it was a bad idea for me to come here?"

Their replies pinged through almost immediately.

"Shut. Up. That is gorgeous!" Mia said.

"Wow! I'll be sure to share these with your grandma!" said my mom.

I dropped my bags and got out my toiletries and headed toward the enormous bathroom. I couldn't get out of my gross travel clothes fast enough. I walked to the black and white checkered-tiled walk-in shower and turned on the water. It poured down from the rainfall showerhead and the pressure was amazing. I almost squealed with delight as I got in.

"Mmm," I moaned a little bit, standing under the water as I felt my shoulders fully relax. I was careful to keep my mouth closed so I didn't drink the water, but no matter what, I was here! I made it! I was doing the thing, and in a little while I'd be having my very first dinner in la Ciudad de Mexíco.

CHAPTER THREE
La Ciudad de Mexico

Waking up to my alarm the next morning, my head thumped with the dull ache of a hangover. It felt naïve to have doubted how smoothly tequila in Mexico City would go down. So many margaritas. So much celebrating.

In my mind I could still hear the revelry from the dinner the night before. Everyone talking excitedly about all the things they wanted to do and see. Passing plates of delicious food around the table, toasting to everything fantastic we tried, toasting to our generous servers who brought us flan on the house at the end of the meal, toasting to our deal and our impending success, toasting to Charles, who would be retiring after we closed this deal. It was a bonding moment for the team, but I was paying for it this morning.

I rolled over and groaned slightly, pulling the pillow back over my head. Six-thirty in the morning and time to get to work. My mouth was dry, and I reached for the water bottle on the nightstand. I drank the entire thing in a few gulps and then got up to try and find some Advil from my toiletry kit.

"Make it stop!" I pleaded as I poured out two of the round terracotta-colored pills into my hand. I swallowed them with more water then hopped into the shower to try and make myself feel a bit more normal.

When I got out of the shower, I reached for my toothbrush and on the counter were several bottles of water with a little note that read: *para lavarse los dientes*. To brush your teeth with.

Once clean, I did my hair and makeup, got dressed and checked my phone. I expected to see a text from my parents making sure I'd arrived safely, but I only had messages in the group thread for our team. Some pictures from the night before had been sent to everyone, and there were a few texts from Jake, who had jumped into an unofficial leadership position, since he spoke Spanish. He wanted everyone down in the lobby by seven-thirty so we could get in our cars and head to the office. I grabbed my work bag and took a look around the room to check if I'd left anything, then with a nod of confidence, I headed out the door and toward the elevator bank.

As I walked into the lobby, I saw my team congregating around a group of sofas. Everyone was holding coffee cups.

Max handed one to me. "Chai latte?"

"Thank you," I reached for it gratefully and took a long sip. We piled into black sedans and headed toward Global Core's Mexico City office.

Even though it was early in the morning, the streets were crowded. There were honking cars weaving in and out of lanes... there might as well have been no lanes. In the daylight, I could see how truly massive the city was. It stretched on for miles and miles. Everywhere I looked there were buildings and way off in the distance were the Sierra Madre mountains. I sipped on my chai latte and felt the painkillers kick in. The combination, mixed with my rising adrenaline and excitement, was working to diminish the power of my hangover.

After more than an hour in traffic, the black sedans pulled up to a huge glass building in the middle of the business district. As we slowed, Max looked over at me and raised his eyebrows playfully.

"Here we go," he said. "Ready?"

"Si, señor," I replied.

We departed the car much in the same way that we had the night before, staring up in awe. It was still hard for me to believe that we were actually here. The experience still felt very surreal. "We'll be meeting the Mexico City team this morning," Jake's voice interrupted my reverie and snapped me back to attention.

"Blake, I'm hoping that you will help us be an intermediary between our team and the Mexico City team. Aside from me, you're our most fluent Spanish speaker so I'll be tapping you in for certain assignments with them."

"Right," Charles chimed in as well. "They will be hosting us to a degree so it's important and that we give them our best. We don't want to impose on them by expecting them to do all of their work in English to accommodate us. Understood?"

The rest of us nodded in agreement.

"Do they speak any English?" George asked.

"Yes, but I think they'll be more comfortable working in Spanish," Jake said. "So, that's where Blake and I will come in, to translate for our team when necessary."

My excitement grew at the idea of speaking Spanish to help my team. That alone made me feel less like the new girl and more like a helpful member of the group.

We walked into the lobby of the building to check in at the security desk. They took our ID's and issued us each security badges. Then we were instructed to take the elevator up to the 44th floor where we'd find Global Core's offices.

When we exited the elevator, we checked in with the front desk receptionist, who completed more security checks by confirming employment before showing us around. The space was beautiful—giant glass windows showing all of Mexico City, as well as views of the mountains. I walked over to some of the windows and stared out at the view, rooted to the spot for a few moments.

"Blake, you coming?" Max called to me. The rest of the team had moved on.

"Sorry," I said, turning to catch up. "But can you believe this view?"

"Don't worry," George said. "You'll be sick of it by the time we're done here."

We settled into our workspace. Global Core had designated one office for the PacSouth/Timbre deal team to work in as well as a conference room with a large table. We walked into the conference room, ready to meet the rest of our team. There were several boxes of traditional Mexican pastries and a few carafes of coffee, but no other team members.

"Where's the rest of them?" I asked Charles, confused.

"I'm sure they'll be here any moment," Jake said confidently. We made ourselves comfortable and helped ourselves to some breakfast as we waited. I took the opportunity to take out my laptop and get set up at the table. I retrieved the briefing documents that we'd be going over with the Mexico team and got out a notepad and a pen.

"It's like the first day of school huh, Blake?" George teased me. "You got a TI-83 calculator and pencil case too?"

"Very funny, George," I responded with a laugh. "I get it. You guys are gonna tease me a little bit, but don't worry, I can take it, I grew up with three boys, so I have thick skin."

"It's all in good fun," he said to me. "We're all very glad you're here. The only thing I can say in Spanish is, más cervezas, por favor."

"Don't kid yourself," I replied, conspiratorially. "That's a very important phrase to know. And I'm sure you'll pick up more along the way."

"Here's hoping!" George reached over and high fived me.

By nine-forty-five, the rest of the team still hadn't shown up and Jake was starting to get worried. He went to the front desk to see if anyone had any information, but it seemed that they knew as much as we did.

We sat around the table, continuing our own administrative work to get ourselves better prepared. We organized our files, our calendars, formatted slides and discussed our plan of attack for the week. I sent a couple of emails to my family back home, as well as Mia, checking in. Occasionally, I nibbled on some of the leftover Concha pastries. Jake was pacing around the room checking his phone. His brow was furrowed, and he was mumbling to himself as he walked back and forth between our desks and the bank of windows. Occasionally he'd meander over to Charles and say something to him under his breath.

I glanced around at George and Max, but they both had their heads down, working. The tension was high, and nobody dared say anything.

Finally, around eleven o'clock the rest of the team arrived, two women, and a man. Jake leapt out of his seat to speak with them as soon as they arrived. In Spanish, he greeted them and then asked if everything was okay. They answered back that they had been stuck in traffic.

"For three hours?" I mumbled to myself. I saw Max smile to himself. He must have heard me.

Jake mentioned in Spanish that our team had been in the office since eight-thirty and then asked if he had gotten the meeting time wrong. I watched the Mexico team members' faces as Jake spoke.

They looked confused and one of the women looked like she might start laughing.

"Lo siento," said the man. "This is the Mexico City way!"

"Were you really expecting us to come in that early?" the woman who appeared to be stifling a laugh asked in Spanish.

"Yes," Jake answered. "But it's fine you're here now, let's just get started."

With that, Jake began the meeting in English, occasionally translating into Spanish if he saw any confused faces from the Mexico team members. He asked them to introduce themselves. In broken English, they each greeted us. The man was Ricardo, he was a consultant, the same level as Max. He had a sort of portly physique and a larger-than-life smile that immediately put me at ease. The shorter-haired woman, who I found out would serve as my day-to-day lead was Chela. She seemed timid and behind her full face of makeup, she looked exhausted, and her eyes were filled with sadness. Finally, there was their manager, Lola. She was the one who had been stifling a laugh. She was Polly-Pocket sized, but she had an assertive energy to her. My intuition told me that there was a fire in her and she was not to be underestimated.

We greeted them all, but it was clear that there was still a bit of tension in the air with the language barriers as well as the confusing start to the day. You could feel a bit of natural skepticism floating above the conference room table. Each side seemed to be evaluating the other. I hoped that this would dissipate. We were going to be working long hours together to finalize the merger and it is always the hope that you'd gel with your new co-workers, if for no other reason than to be productive, and get the work done without issue.

Jake jumped in again, immediately highlighting the key clients and the strong relationships that we have established in the U.S. "This is a priority client for our firm," he explained. "There is the potential for more acquisitions in Latin America, so we need to do what we can to over-deliver for Timbre and PacSouth. If we get this right, we could all make our careers here and there will be more work for years to come."

Charles spoke then. "I know we got off to a rough start this morning, but let's put that behind us and do our best work." He had a way of defusing tension, and I felt the room relax a bit at his words. "Each of you have been hand-picked for this project based on your previous experience. The U.S. team is bringing their expertise in mergers and acquisitions and client relationships. The Mexico team has extensive knowledge of telecom, the Grupo Merced client and how things work here in Mexico. We need each of you to work together to make sure you are bringing the best of Global Core Consulting to our client."

I looked around. Everyone at the table was smiling tentatively and nodding. It seemed like maybe we were back on track.

"Great! Let's keep going," George chimed in.

Jake looked satisfied. "Alright, let's take a look at some of the key players. George, do you want to lead this?" Jake asked, as he opened his laptop and connected it to the presentation screen in the room.

"Absolutely," George stood up and moved toward the presentation screen. The first face appeared on the screen. "Let's discuss the team that we'll be in negotiations with. First up, we have Carlos Ruiz," he said. "Carlos will be moving here shortly from the U.S. to ensure the integration between Timbre and PacSouth goes smoothly."

"That's right!" Jake added. "He's a good guy and he's grown up at PacSouth. He's risen up the corporate ladder quickly, so this is a great opportunity for him. We want to make sure we make him successful especially with the team in the U.S."

More nodding around the table. Some of the team was taking notes. Jake pressed the spacebar on his laptop and the next face flashed on the presentation screen.

"Efrain Gallego will be our key client from Timbre and our day-to-day lead on the client side," George said. "He will be working closely with Carlos and Carlos wants updates from us on Efrain's progress as they have never worked together."

The next face clicked into view, and I felt the tension in the room rise. "Tomas Barajas is the head of Grupo Merced," Jake explained. "He is a tough businessman, and we need to be sure we're always a step ahead of him."

"Doesn't he own Club Mexico, the fútbol team?" Ricardo asked.

"I believe so," Chela confirmed.

"Football?" George asked.

"Soccer," Lola corrected. "He has many business endeavors."

She spat out the last word and it was evident that she had an opinion of Tomas that wasn't very favorable.

"Lola, are you familiar with any of these men?" Jake asked. "¿Los Conoces?"

"Solo por su reputación," Lola answered coldly. "Él no es un hombre bueno. Necesitamos tener cuidado con las personas de Grupo Merced. No tengo confienza en ellos."

Max and George looked at me. "She said, only by reputation," I whispered to him. "And that we should be careful with the members of Grupo Merced."

The room was quiet and then Ricardo broke the ice. "There are a lot of rumors. But we don't really know for sure. He could be an honorable businessman."

"Honorable?" Lola asked looking for clarification and as Ricardo explained to them in Spanish, both Lola and Chela began to laugh and shake their heads leaving me with a giant pit in my stomach.

"Alright, let's move on," Jake said, eager to continue. "Thank you, George."

"No problem," George said, finding his seat again. "I know you all received briefs on the deal, but now that we're all together I want to make sure we all understand what we're doing here. There are a lot of moving parts, and we have some newer team members with us." He looked at me and I forced a smile. "Our US client, PacSouth, has bought a division of Grupo Merced and that's Timbre. Usually in deals like this we would have more time upfront to do due diligence and develop the Transitional Service Agreements (TSAs) to support the Timbre team during the integration time frame. However, because the deal closed so quickly there wasn't time for that and now, we're going to have to hustle a bit to ensure the transition is smooth."

"And what does that mean exactly?" Ricardo asked.

"It means that we have to negotiate the terms of the TSA for Timbre, so they can keep operations running smoothly until they're fully integrated into PacSouth."

"Essentially, Timbre has split off from Grupo Merced," George stood up and walked over to the white board. He began drawing a diagram to demonstrate. "But the people, processes and technology are still very much intertwined. Grupo Merced is required to provide services like payroll processing, network tower maintenance, and financial accounting until PacSouth can stand up all processes and technology requirements to support Timbre themselves. That is why they are called Transitional Service Agreements as they should only be in place for a short amount of time. There's going to be an integration period, where Timbre moves from one parent company to another."

"Kind of like my parents' divorce—splitting up assets and moving homes," Max joked.

"Right, and our job is to identify any gaps from a people, process, and technology perspective, and identify the correct cost for the services being provided," said Jake. "In essence, identifying people cost and technology cost."

"So, we're negotiating the cost on PacSouth's behalf and developing a plan to help them exit the TSAs as quickly as possible," I interjected.

George looked pleased. "That's right, Blake."

"Look at you, new kid!" Max nudged me. Lola turned to face me. I smiled at her, but her eyes narrowed, and her stare was so intense that it sent chills down my spine. *Yikes.*

"We have a kick-off meeting with the Timbre and PacSouth team tomorrow," Jake said. "So, we need to finalize our kick-off materials, begin developing our templates to capture the TSA requirements and the cost associated with them as well as begin developing our project plan. George and Blake, can you put the finishing touches on the kick-off deck? Once done, I want to talk through roles and responsibilities during the meeting tomorrow."

"No problem," I said.

"We're on it," George added.

"Chela and Max, can you start working through some of the templates and requirements for the teams coming out of the meeting tomorrow?"

"Okay," Chela said timidly.

"I can help with any translation challenges," Ricardo added.

"Sounds great," said Max.

"Lola, Ricardo and I will work to define the detailed project plan for the next three months," Jake said. "Let's reconvene before the end of the day to discuss next steps."

After a very long first day, Charles insisted that we have dinner together to continue getting to know each other. We left the Global Core offices and headed out for a team dinner at one of Mexico City's most popular restaurants, Pujol.

I had spent some time reading up on Chef Enrique Olvera and his menu of traditional Mexican dishes with a Japanese twist and as we walked into the sleek restaurant, an anticipatory grin spread across my face.

We were seated at a large table and noticed that there were no menus on the table and looked at each other confused. "I've asked the chef to bring us a special tasting, off menu. He's a friend," said Lola.

"How marvelous!" Charles exclaimed. "Gracias, Lola."

"De nada," Lola said. She looked proud.

The servers returned with pitchers of different flavors of margaritas for us to try. There was chili yuzu, tamarind, avocado leaf and even prickly pear. They smelled amazing and after the long day of working with a hangover, I gladly reached for a little hair of the dog.

"I think we should have a toast," boasted Jake, as George filled glasses with each of our preferences.

"Great idea!" said Ricardo. "I'm excited to finally have our team together!"

Once everyone had a glass in their hand, Lola cleared her throat, commanding attention. "Salud, amor, y dinero. ¡Y tiempo para gastarlo!"

We all raised our glasses. "¡Salud!"

Charles looked at Lola. "I have no idea what you just said but it sounds like something I could toast to—health, money..." He trailed off unsure what the rest of the words meant.

Lola jumped in. "Health, love and money. And time to enjoy it all!"

"Amazing." George said. "I will need to bring that back to the U.S. with me."

We all cheered in unison.

As the evening moved on, the team seemed to be getting along better and better. Maybe it was the drinks. Maybe it was the plates of delicious food that kept coming to the table. There were seafood tostadas with daikon and nori, fish tacos with avocado, seaweed, Mexican mint, and kimchi. My favorites were the tamales with plantain, and the tacos with grilled octopus, which kind of freaked George out. We all cheered him on as he tried one.

"¿Cómo se dice 'not too bad' en Español?" he asked Chela, after his first bite.

"You can just say, está bien," she replied, with a laugh.

"Well then, ¡Está bien!" he said.

"Yay George!" I exclaimed, raising my glass. Everyone else toasted to George with me.

The hours passed and we all fell easily into conversation. I chatted with Chela a bit about what it was like living in Mexico City. She loved it, although she said she had dreams of moving to the states, maybe to Los Angeles. Max, an LA native, heard this and joined our conversation. Ricardo and George were deep into a discussion about American football, Ricardo was a huge Dallas Cowboys fan. I watched Charles, Jake, and Lola chatting. Lola seemed to have relaxed significantly. She talked about vacation destinations she wanted to visit in the Caribbean. The sounds of chatter and laughter around the table warmed my heart and by the end of the dinner, it felt like our team was ready to go into battle together.

I reached into my bag and pulled out my phone. I sent a quick text message to Mia. "Our Mexico team is really great! At our first team dinner now! Lots of margs and amazing food! Off to a good start!"

She responded right away. "Yay! Anyone cute?"

I shook my head, laughed, and replied back to her. "I don't date colleagues, remember?"

"Never say never!" she said. "xoxo!"

CHAPTER FOUR
El Taxi

The next morning, I had gotten the routine. Hot shower, a couple of Advil, followed by a warm beverage.

"I don't think I can keep drinking tequila every night!" I said to Max as we got into the car.

"I hear you." He had his sunglasses on and as he took a sip of coffee, his hands shook a little bit.

Aside from the slight hangover, part dos, I felt confident and excited going into our second day of work, but when we arrived at the office the next morning, neither Chela, Ricardo, nor Lola were there, and Jake went into a little bit of a panic again.

"How are we supposed to work like this?" Jake complained to Charles. "The kick-off meeting is at noon!"

"We have to expect some cultural differences here, Jake," I heard Charles reply in a hushed tone. "These people are hosting us; we'd be smart to adapt to their schedules. Take a load off, have a pastry." Those were words I never anticipated hearing from Charles, and I could tell Jake was surprised as well. In true Jake fashion, he followed directions by picking up a pastry but instead of relaxing he kept pushing forward.

Lola came in around ten o'clock, and Jake looked relieved, so I counted that as a win, but Ricardo and Chela arrived just before noon, and I could tell that everyone was a bit nervous to have such a short amount of time before we'd start the kick-off meeting. The vein in Jake's temple seemed to be visibly pulsing.

George moved around the space frantically trying to distribute information packets. Charles was trying to be our calm, fearless leader but even he looked like he'd broken a bit of a sweat. I felt my stomach twist into a knot.

"We're gonna have to sort this out with them before we move into negotiations," I overheard George whisper to Jake as we watched Chela and Ricardo get settled.

As soon as the teams from PacSouth and Timbre started to arrive, the vibe in the conference room got exponentially more tense. I noticed a lot of hushed voices and sideways glances between all the people in the room. The knot in my stomach tightened. This was the first time that all the teams were meeting and as far as I understood it was the first time either company had dealt with an international merger.

The Timbre people looked unsettled and anxious, and I imagined most of them were unsure about what the merger meant for their jobs and their futures.

Looking around, I realized that Chela, Lola, and I were the only women in the meeting, and I noted the fact that I seemed to be at least ten years younger than anyone in the room.

Jake and George began with introductions in English, their demeanor having changed entirely as soon as they were on. It was almost as if they were puffing out their chests to make themselves seem more formidable in a room full of rather intense looking men.

I stood in the back, taking notes. There was an unavoidable hiccup-pattern to the flow of the meeting. Whenever our team spoke in English, the Mexican translators for the Timbre employees would have to translate the statements for them. Or if Jake was speaking, he'd try to do both. There were delays before we could move on. Poor George, Charles and Max were left to fend for themselves in trying to decipher the things that were discussed in Spanish, but Jake and I had agreed to clue them in later, so part of my job was to write down the key points that they'd need.

Eventually, Efrain was introduced, and he shared how excited everyone at Timbre was to merge with PacSouth.

"We really feel that this is a new beginning for all of us at Timbre, and we're looking forward to the future!" He talked intently about opportunities to grow as a company and as individual employees. There was a smattering of applause around the room, but when I glanced at the Timbre team, they seemed only moderately enthusiastic.

Eventually Carlos was introduced, and he spoke about his experience coming up the ranks at PacSouth. "I've been passionate about this company since I began work here almost ten years ago," he said. "I know through time and experience you will find joy and value of working here. And I know together with Timbre we will be even more successful as a company and on a global scale."

He went on, speaking with a lot of enthusiasm as he punctuated his statements in English with Spanish translations. Passing around packets to the Timbre team that provided an overview of PacSouth, he explained how Timbre would fit into their long-term strategic vision and how important the market in Mexico was to their U.S. market and their customers. At this point there seemed to be an ease in the tension on the Timbre side.

Then it was our turn. Our team stood up and walked to the front. There wasn't really a need for all of us to be up there with Jake and George, but I think they wanted us to be visible to all the Timbre and PacSouth members.

"Over the next few months," Jake began. "We will be here to support Timbre as you transition from Grupo Merced to your new home at PacSouth." He took a moment to translate into Spanish and there was another smattering of applause.

"During the transition period," George began. "We will be here to facilitate meetings with Grupo Merced and ensure that Timbre has all of the key requirements in place to be successful in the short term while we work to stand the Timbre team up on PacSouth systems and processes."

"Next, we will be hosting individual breakout sessions with each of the teams from Timbre," said Jake. "IT, Network Infrastructure, HR, Finance, Legal and Customer Service. So, we can answer any additional questions you might have."

Everyone in the room shifted as we prepared to move into breakout sessions. After a while, lunch was brought in by the Global Core staff and we continued our work until the sun was going down.

By the time the Timbre and PacSouth people left, I was thoroughly exhausted. After hours of breakout sessions, we gathered again, just our team, to discuss next steps and debrief on the meetings. I gave copies of my notes to Charles, George, and Max, and then we went over them.

It seemed the most challenging element of the merger was going to relate to the network towers for Timbre. Ricardo was an expert in this field, and he informed us that we might run into some problems. "A lot of the network towers are located in lands that are heavily operated by the cartel," he said. "So, we need to be very mindful of how we handle this."

It was sobering to be reminded of where we were and the realities of the political dynamics in Mexico. It was an element to this deal that I realized I wasn't fully prepared for. I had read up on the cartels in Mexico but reading an article online and facing the reality of it in real time was a totally different story.

As the workday came to a close, Jake went over a list of final tasks we needed to achieve before we wrapped for the day.

"Blake, I need you and Max to go to Timbre's offices at Grupo Merced and pick up some documents for tomorrow's meetings. We'll meet you at the hotel afterwards."

"No problem," Max said.

He and I packed up our stuff for the day and eventually headed down to the lobby. Max called us an Uber on his phone, and we headed across town to the Timbre and Grupo Merced offices.

I enjoyed the car ride, taking in more views of the city. I was starting to be able to recognize landmarks now and that excited me. There was a large Mexican flag, that looked like the size of a football field on the side of the freeway. There was a large square building with a smaller circular building on top of it. It was the largest building around for what seemed like miles. I asked our Uber driver what was up there in Spanish. He responded "Este edificio es el World Trade Center de Mexico y hay un resteraunte muy boinita se llama Bellini."

"Gracias, Señor." I took note and added Bellini to my Mexico City bucket list.

Traveling around the city reminded me of when I first moved to Dallas from Southern California. There was something invigorating about beginning to learn and understand a new city. It was a feeling I was very familiar with. My family moved a lot when I was growing up, and while it added some challenges to my social life, it made me highly adaptable.

Max and I secured the documents from Timbre and walked back outside just as a light rain began to fall. He handed the paperwork to me as he pulled his phone back out to call us another Uber back to the hotel.

"Shit," he muttered. "There are no cars available right now."

"What?" I asked. "No way, that can't be right."

"Look," he said, showing me his phone. "It says the nearest car is twelve miles away and can be here in forty minutes."

"What should we do?" I asked.

"Call a taxi?" he said.

"Didn't they tell us not to do that? They said Ubers only. Taxi's here aren't always safe." I thought back to my grandma Mary Jo's story.

It was at that time that a man from the lobby walked outside.

"Perdoname, Señor, Señorita...¿Estás perdido? Are you lost?"

"Yes, we're a part of the PacificSouth team, we are trying to find a ride back to our hotel." I responded in Spanish.

"Bienvenida a Grupo Merced. Me Llamo Sam. I work for Tomas Barajas. I can call you a taxi."

Max and I looked at each other. The man looked like he could be trusted, and we were at the Timbre offices.

"Okay..." Max said. "Thank you."

"Don't worry, we'll get you back to your hotel safely." He picked up his phone and put it to his ear.

Within a few minutes our taxi arrived, and we got in. The driver was young and seemed a little distracted.

"¡Hola!" I said as I entered the vehicle. "¿Cómo está, Usted?"

"Bien, gracias," he replied. "¿A dónde vas?"

"The W hotel in Polanco," I replied.

He took off in a bit of a hurry and both Max and I buckled up and reached up for the handles above the windows to hold on.

As he drove along, I watched him peer into the rear-view mirror and make eye contact with us. He seemed nervous. My intuition was telling me something wasn't right. After a few moments I noticed that the car was heading in the opposite direction from where we had come. I pulled out my phone to look up directions back to the hotel, which showed we had now gone about fifteen minutes in the wrong direction. I flashed my screen to Max.

"Excuse me," I said to the driver. "This is the wrong way. Está no es la dirección correcta."

He ignored me. Outside the car the rain started to pick up.

"Sir," Max spoke up. "Please turn around, this is not the way to our hotel." Max and I exchanged a slightly panicked look.

"Max, share our location with Jake," I commanded.

"I am not getting kidnapped and held for ransom like a cliché in some movie," he muttered as he opened his phone.

"¡Señor, para el coche! Stop the car!" I yelled. "¡Ahora!"

He ignored me and kept driving. I watched as his hands tightened around the steering wheel. This was quickly becoming a very unsafe situation. The speed of the vehicle increased, and the driver took a sudden detour on to another highway that was heading east of the city. I knew that tourists had been abducted in taxis in Mexico, but I never imagined that it could happen in broad daylight.

Think, Blake, Think! I tried to think about what would make me want to get someone out of my car as fast as possible. I thought about the last time Mia, and I had been in a cab coming home late from the bars. Mia had been belting out Britney Spears and I could tell the driver was hugely relieved when he dropped us off.

I looked a Max, trying to clue him in to what I was about to do, and then at the top of my lungs I started belting out, "Oops I did it again!!! I played with your heart, got lost in the game!!! Oh baby, baby!"

Max looked at me wide-eyed with raised eyebrows. "Have you lost your mind?!"

"¡Eh! ¡Callate!" The driver shouted at us.

I kept singing and nodded at Max and gestured for him to join me. He rolled his eyes as if he were about to do something hugely embarrassing and then he joined in.

"OH BABY, BABY! OOPS! YOU THINK I'M IN LOVE!!!"

We were screaming in the back of the car on repeat. The car continued to race down the road; my heart was beating out of my chest.

"I'M NOT THAT INNOCENT!!!"

The driver kept shouting at us to be quiet. He looked panicked himself. Max and I ignored him, and we kept singing.

Finally, Max showed me his phone. He'd received a text from Jake. "Lie and tell him the police are on the way. Keep your location services on. We're coming to get you!"

"Señor, la policia sabe nuestro posición!" I yelled to him "Ellos van a estar aqui en algunos minutos. ¡Para el coche ahora!"

"Pinche perra," he muttered under his breath as he slowed the car.

"What did he say?" Max asked as the car stopped.

"It doesn't matter," I replied. "Just get out!"

Max and I jumped out and moved out of the way of traffic. The taxi raced off. Max's phone rang and he picked up. It was Jake.

"He let us out!" he said. "How?! Some crazy white girl shit! Blake started scream-singing Britney Spears and it freaked him out."

Jake and Lola arrived after about fifteen minutes. Both Max's and my clothes were thoroughly soaked from the rain.

"What the hell happened?" Jake asked, as we got in the car.

"Why didn't you call an Uber?"

"There were no Ubers, man!" Max said, shaking water out of his hair. "Some guy at Timbre said he'd call us a cab. We figured it was safe."

"What guy from Timbre?" Lola asked, as she pulled back onto the highway. She looked furious.

"Someone named Sam," I said. "He said he worked for Tomas Barajas."

"Bastardo." Lola sounded disgusted. The car rumbled gently along the highway and the raindrops slid down the windows like tears falling.

Jake immediately picked up his phone and dialed. "Charles, we have a problem."

I couldn't hear what Charles was saying on the other line, but Jake was shaking his head in agreement. "Yes. I agree. Thanks, Charles." He hung up the phone and looked back at us. "We're handling it."

When I got back to my room that night, I was so wired that I had a hard time thinking about going to sleep. I felt like I wanted to tell someone what had happened to me. My parents... but I was terrified to tell them the truth. I knew they'd panic and demand I come home immediately. I tried to take a hot bath and remind myself that nothing had actually happened. We had kept our wits about us, and we'd escaped a situation that could have been bad. It was a reminder to be more vigilant and trust our instincts. I tossed and turned throughout the night and when my alarm went off in the morning, I felt like I had blinked twice and got zero sleep.

I got myself ready, my body was numb, and I felt as if I was watching my own life on a TV screen. I felt defeated and nervous. When I reached for my toothbrush, my hand started to shake. Eventually, I made my way downstairs to meet the team in the lobby. When I got off the elevator, I saw them huddled around someone I didn't recognize. A tall man in a suit with broad shoulders, dark hair, and light green eyes.

He looked like no man I had ever seen before. He was a perfect mix of Jesse Williams, from Grey's Anatomy, and Feliciano Lopez, the Spanish tennis player. He took my breath away he was gorgeous, and I nearly froze at the sight of him.

"Oh Blake, good! You're here," said Jake. "I want you to meet our new security detail."

He reached his hand out to me with a warm smile. "Mucho gusto," he said. "Me llamo Gio."

CHAPTER FIVE
Gio

Once when I was in middle school, my father—a high profile prosecutor, received death threats after one of his cases. As a precaution the city assigned a security guard named Gregory to our family for the duration of the trial, which my brothers and I thought was mostly entertaining. We made grand plans to figure out ways to ditch him, but our mother was always two steps ahead of us and warned him that we might try to pull this kind of stunt.

Gregory was a good guy and eventually he played along when we tried to play 'ditch the security guard.' After a few days, we warmed to him and discovered he was great at basketball. By the end of the trial, we lost our playmate, but I don't think it ever hit home for us that our family could have been in danger.

I hadn't been in any kind of similar situation since that time, and now I could feel my inner-rebellious middle schooler longing not to be supervised, while I also understood it was in my best interest to have this Gio around.

Nevertheless, it still felt odd. Gio accompanied us to the office every day and back to the hotel every evening. He was usually silent, riding quietly along with us in our black town car. He would walk us into the lobby of the hotel and then disappear. But as if by magic, he'd be right there waiting again the next morning, always well dressed and professional.

When we left the hotel grounds to see the sights in the city or go out to eat, he was there. Even on weekends. His quiet demeanor seemed to imply an unspoken understanding of professional distance, and so none of us really spoke to him much. He was just always around, like a shadow.

In the evenings, at the hotel bar, our group speculated about his backstory. George in particular seemed quite interested in his story. "Do you think he's had any run-ins with any of the cartels?" he asked animatedly over margaritas. "Do you think he's killed anyone?"

"Who knows," Charles mused. "I think life as a Mexican citizen is very different from anything that any of us have ever known..."

"He definitely looks like someone you don't want to mess with," Max chimed in.

"And that's why I'm glad he's around," said Jake.

"I do wish he'd say more," I said. The group all stared at me in silence. "What? Why doesn't he want to talk to us? You don't think it's odd that he's so quiet? I keep wondering what he's thinking."

"Oh yeah, Blake? You want to get inside Gio's head?" Max teased me.

"Stop it, Max," I laughed. "I just wish he'd acknowledge us more, we are people, we're more than a job."

"You're blushing a little bit," said George.

"Okay, y'all are being highly unprofessional!" I teased them. "Now someone get me another margarita."

"Yes ma'am," Max laughed and raised his hand to signal our waitress.

Sometimes having Gio around made me feel more worried, because it meant that the client felt we needed to have someone around to protect us, and that made me uneasy, which I mused was the opposite of his intended effect. And I knew if my family found out we had a security guard they would push me to come home immediately. Either way, I had some mixed emotions about having Gio around.

My own curiosities about Gio began to spike one Sunday when our team went to visit the main plaza in Mexico City, El Zócalo. At some point during the afternoon, I made a comment to the group that I was going to find a bathroom and Gio followed me there and positioned himself outside the door.

"Is this necessary?" I said before I could stop myself.

"Keeping you safe is my job," he replied in perfect English. He was stern and a little cold when he spoke which left me stunned as no one had spoken to me that way before. I couldn't find the words to reply. Instead, I just exhaled and walked into the restroom.

I splashed a little cold water on my neck. Even though it was winter, it was still warm and humid outside, and I felt a bit flushed. "Keep it together, Blake," I scolded myself in the mirror.

As I walked out of the bathroom I looked to where Gio had been standing, but he wasn't there. For an instant I panicked thinking something had happened to him, but I quickly shrugged that notion away, remembering his sheer size. What could possibly happen to him on a busy street in the middle of the day?

I walked down the street a little bit back to where I knew my friends were waiting and that was when I saw him, standing with his back to me. I was about to call out to him, but there was something in his posture and the tone with which he was speaking that stopped me.

"Sam, no. No puedo," he said. "Sabes que no puedo. Esa ya no es mi vida." *You know I can't. That's not my life anymore.*

"Sam?" I said to myself. "It couldn't be..." Suddenly I felt very uncomfortable thinking that it could the same Sam from Grupo Merced. I felt like I was hearing something very personal that I shouldn't be privy to. Gio sounded panicked. He sounded vulnerable. It was disarming. I waited another moment before I said anything.

"Gio?" I called. He started and turned to me. "I'm ready."

"Tengo que ir," he said into the phone before hanging up. "Sorry about that," he said to me.

"That's okay," I said. "Your wife?" I attempted a joke. "Is she mad that you work so much?"

It worked. He laughed. "No, no, nothing like that," he said. "And I'm a bachelor, as you Americans say. Like the guy with all the roses."

"Ah, so you're more of a player then?" I shot back.

"No, no not like that." He responded nervously.

Together we laughed. And we walked side by side back to the group.

As we moved ahead with the Timbre deal, Gio's presence started to feel a little bit more normal, as if he was just another part of the team. Each day he would nod at me and smile as I'd come down to the lobby.

"Good morning," he'd say, cordially.

"Good morning," I'd reply.

He was perfectly pleasant, but there were moments when we made eye contact that left me feeling a little self-conscious. I found myself fixing my hair and checking my reflection before I encountered him in the morning. I didn't know why I felt this way, but I knew that Gio seemed to watch me with a curiosity that I had a hard time figuring out.

We began to follow Ricardo, Lola, and Chela's lead and have two-hour lunches in the middle of our workdays, especially if there was a fútbol game on they wanted to watch. It was an activity that made me feel completely uncomfortable at the start, like I was shirking my responsibilities and being lazy, but eventually, Chela encouraged me to let go.

"Relax, Blake. You are in Mexico!" she said. "Try to enjoy your time here. The work will still be there when we get back to the office."

And so, on a Wednesday in the middle of February, over al pastor tacos and micheladas, I finally learned the truth about Gio.

Most days during lunch he sat away from our table or at the far end of the table near Ricardo, but on this day in particular he chose a seat next to George and directly across from me.

"Is it okay to sit here?" he asked me.

"Of course!" George jumped in.

Gio glanced to his left at Ricardo who gave a little laugh.

"George wants to know your whole story," said Ricardo. "He's fascinated."

George looked slightly embarrassed but conceded. "It's true," he said. "We don't know all that much about you, Gio. And you're part of the team now."

I glanced at Jake who raised his eyebrows and shrugged his shoulders as if to say, *what can ya do?*

"It's okay if you don't want to share though," Charles chimed in. "We don't want to pry."

At that moment the servers arrived with our food and there was a halt to our conversation as we each accepted our plates and thanked them. I thought this would put an end to the discussion but as soon as we were settled, Gio spoke.

"It's alright," he said, evenly. "I am happy to share."

"Are you from Mexico City?" Chela asked.

"I'm from Puebla," he replied. "We are known in Mexico because we are the only town that celebrates Cinco de Mayo."

This confused me. I looked around at the rest of my team and they looked confused too. "I thought Cinco de Mayo was kind of a national celebration," I said.

"A common belief," he said.

I felt my cheeks get hot. "Oh, sorry."

"It's nothing to apologize for," he replied. "Most Americans don't know the true story of Cinco de Mayo."

"And now you're going to tell us, eh?" Lola teased him.

"Si, claro," Gio said with a smile. "Mexico has a very complicated history. We fought for a long time to gain our independence from Spain, and then we had a war with the United States and later a civil war amongst ourselves. Basically, you could say there was a little bit of uhh drama."

"Just a little bit," added Ricardo with a wry smile. Everyone at the table laughed, charmed.

"After all of this, the economy was ruined so our country borrowed money from England, Spain and France," Gio continued. "It took us a long time to pay it back and there came a point where Mexico needed a couple more years to get more money together as they couldn't pay. England and Spain seemed to understand this, or they didn't want to have another war, but the French were not as understanding. So, they came to put pressure on us, and they invaded the city of Puebla, my hometown. This of course happened on Cinco de Mayo of that year."

"The French thought that the people of Puebla would surrender easily and that they could overthrow the Guadalupe Fortress, but the people of Puebla were strong and determined and we fought them off. In the end, the French retreated and lost nearly five-hundred men, and we lost less than one hundred. The

General named Zaragoza was said to be a hero and they renamed the city Puebla de Zaragoza. There was a whole lot more fighting after that... but eventually Mexico was fully independent, and Benito Juarez reclaimed the presidency and named Cinco de Mayo a holiday. Now, in the city of Puebla every year on Cinco de Mayo, the people reenact the battle and then they drink and party."

George looked enraptured. "Wow," he gushed. "What was it like growing up in a town with so much rich history and culture?"

"It was normal," said Gio, and I couldn't help but crack a smile. He caught my eye for a split second, and I felt some kind of electric current buzzing in my stomach.

"And your family, what are they like?" I blurted out.

"They are great. It's my mom, sisters, and me. When I was eighteen, my father passed and as the oldest I quit school to help take care of my family, eventually I found myself working for Grupo Merced, but I recently left due to some... differences in opinion on how to do my job."

"What does that mean?" I asked.

"I actually can't tell you that," he replied. "I signed a non-disclosure agreement with them."

"But you don't work for them anymore..." I hedged. "Doesn't that mean your NDA is terminated?"

Gio turned to Ricardo and mumbled to him, "Dios mío. Ella hace muchas preguntas."

"I ask a lot of questions because I want to learn. Especially about our current client." I said to him. He turned to face me again, looking a little stunned. "What? Nadie expecta que la rubia puede hablar Español."

Jake turned to Max, Charles, and George to translate, "No one expects the blonde girl to speak Spanish."

The team all burst into laughter. Gio threw up his hands as if to say, *touché!* "You're right, they don't!" he said. "Forgive me, Blake."

"We'll see," I said, shaking my head and chuckling.

CHAPTER SIX
Grupo Merced

Returning to the Timbre offices I felt a mixture of emotions. As we entered the building, I glanced at the curbside area where Max and I had gotten in the infamous taxi just a few weeks before. My heart rate increased, and my palms began to sweat. I looked at Max and he looked equally uneasy.

"You good?" I asked him.

"Yeah," he said. "It's just weird."

I could feel my heart racing. I still felt out of place in these big meetings, and it didn't help matters that I was already anxious returning to the scene of the crime. It was obvious that everyone else had so much more experience, but I did my best to be as helpful and proactive as possible and worked hard to ensure I did not get in the way. I took a few deep breaths to settle myself. My lungs struggling to expand as my anxiety gripped them. I looked over to Gio and he gave me a smile with a concerned tilt of the head. I nodded at him to let him know I was okay.

Eventually the Timbre team arrived and greeted us. We went around the table shaking hands and introducing ourselves. Efrain took a moment to introduce us to some of the key players who would be involved in upcoming meetings. Then he sat down and allowed us to proceed.

Jake was the first to speak, explaining in Spanish that we needed to be ready for Grupo Merced to play hardball. "Ustedes no lo harán fácil," he said. *They won't make it easy.*

Efrain and his team looked as though they were expecting to hear this but still weren't pleased. At this point Lola jumped in and said that it was our job to do everything in our power to make sure their team would be set up for success during the transition.

As the meeting proceeded in Spanish, I did my best to translate quietly for George, Charles, and Max. We had worked out a system where I would type what was being said in a document and they could glance at the computer to read it. Charles and George were nodding along calmly but Max still looked a bit uneasy being back at Timbre. He kept glancing over his shoulder to make sure that Gio was still outside the conference room.

"Will we still have access to our key personnel files?" asked one of the women on the Timbre team.

"Yes," said Lola.

"Well, you will for a period of time," Jake interjected. "But once you officially transition to PacSouth, you will likely lose access unless we negotiate with Grupo Merced that you must retain access to documents. In the meantime, I would recommend downloading any key documents that you need to ensure you have them once you no longer have access to the Grupo Merced Systems. We can begin tracking the required documents to ask Grupo Merced for, but we have to be prepared for them not to share."

Some of the team members looked relieved while others jotted down a few quick notes.

Lola's brows were furrowed, and her eyes narrowed. She took a breath. "We will fight for you to ensure that you will not feel the transition of the merger at all." She was impassioned as she spoke, it was exciting to see a strong, forceful woman in control of a room full of males.

At this point Jake interrupted to suggest we break for lunch. He seemed nervous for Lola to make any additional promises to the Timbre team that we weren't entirely sure we could keep. The team moved into a room where a buffet had been set up with a variety of food options and there were tables and chairs where everyone could sit and eat.

My stomach was still feeling a little tight and I wasn't very hungry. I made my way to Gio to see if he wanted to join me for a coffee down in the lobby. I figured he'd follow me down there anyway, if I left the group, so it made the most sense to treat it like an invite.

"Hey," I said. "Would you like to join me for a coffee downstairs?"

"Sure," he said.

"Does anyone else want coffee?" I looked at the rest of the group and everyone shook their heads.

George responded, "I'll take a latte if you are going."

"You got it," I replied.

"You two have fun," George said with a wink. I quickly turned around and pretended like I didn't hear him.

Together we rode the elevator down to the lobby where there was a coffee shop. It was exciting just he and I standing together. I felt highly aware of my body, and also highly aware of the fact that neither of us were speaking. I could smell his cologne. I could feel a hint of warmth coming from his body. I wanted to think of something to say, something clever, something endearing, but my mind was drawing a total blank.

The elevator reached the ground floor and we walked out into the lobby toward the coffee shop.

Finally, he broke our silence, and the relief was palpable. "So...how are the meetings going?" he asked.

"I think okay," I said. "We're still in the initial phases."

"Grupo Merced will be tough," he said.

"Can you give me any inside information?" I attempted a joke.

"I could, but I'd have to kill you," he said, smiling.

We turned the corner and entered the coffee shop when he stopped suddenly. Another man seemed to recognize him and waved. As we got closer, I realized I recognized him too. It was Sam.

My heart started to hammer in my chest, and I had the impulse to get away from him as soon as possible. Gio must have noticed because he gently put his hand on my back to steady me.

"Gio!" He reached out his hand. "¿Cómo estás?"

"Sam." Gio avoided the handshake. "Bien, gracias."

Gio's hand on my back gestured me away from Sam and toward the counter to place our order. I looked up at Gio and he pulled his hand away as if he wasn't sure if he'd crossed a boundary. I smiled and he returned my smile, looking relieved. I felt relieved until I heard Sam's voice again.

"Wait," he said in English. "Aren't you going to introduce me to your friend?"

"Not today," Gio clipped back, and we walked away.

"Oh, we've met," I said to Sam, surprising myself with my own boldness. "You called a cab for my colleague and I. Remember?"

"Ah, yes. La rubia de Global Core." There was a smug smile on his face. I immediately wanted to slap it right off him. "I'd be happy to call another car for you anytime."

"That won't be necessary after what happened last time," I said.

Sam looked me up and down as if he were sizing me up, then he cocked his head to the side as if confused. "I'm not sure I know what you are talking about."

"Well, I know what she's talking about," Gio said. "And we'll be going now.

We walked up to the counter to order, and I felt a little bit stunned. Gio ordered coffees for him and me and the latte for George. Then we walked over to a table in the corner of the coffee shop and sat down.

"Okay, I need some answers," I said. Gio gestured for me to lower my voice slightly and glanced around us. I felt my eyebrows tighten in frustration. "Who is Sam? And how do you know him? And more importantly why do you think he called a cab that appeared to be attempting to kidnap Max and me? None of this makes sense."

"Sam is Tomas' right-hand man. He's the liaison between Timbre and Grupo Merced," he said. "I really don't know what happened with the cab. It could have been intentional; it could have just been a rogue taxi driver hoping to get lucky ransoming two Americans. It's hard to say. But Sam won't bother you again. Trust me."

"How do you know that?"

"It's my job to know that, Blake."

"Gio, this situation with the taxi was clearly serious enough to merit someone like you coming and joining our team. Sam is the one who called us the cab and now you're telling me that he works with Tomas Barajas. The man who we are currently in negotiations with! You think this is all pure coincidence?"

"Blake, please lower your voice," he said in a hushed tone.

"I am the one who got Max and I out of that cab. It's my life that may or may not have been in danger. I don't like being kept in the dark."

"We can discuss this at a later time," he said, standing up. "George is waiting for his latte." There was an edge to his voice that made it very clear that the discussion was over.

But I could feel in my gut that something was off. It reminded me of the way I felt when I had observed Gio on the phone at El Zócalo. There was more to Sam than Gio was letting on and it seemed clear that he didn't want me to know any more.

The next day we had additional meetings with the Timbre team as we dug further into the merger. Jake and Max were spending the day working with the IT function, so that left George and Charles to supervise our meeting teams. Ricardo, Charles, and Chela worked with one group, while Lola, George and I worked with the other.

"Blake, follow my lead in there, okay?" Lola said as we walked into one of the other rooms.

"Yeah, no problem," I said. My stomach felt a little bit uneasy going in.

Lola was a bit of a question mark. It was hard to tell if she was cold or just direct. She didn't smile very much, and she didn't engage with the team. It wasn't something I was accustomed to dealing with. I lived in Texas where everyone was friendly, and I had no problem talking with strangers. I was used to getting along with most people, but it was difficult to talk to Lola. I had tried to chat with her a few times during breaks or meetings, but she had an air of someone that couldn't possibly be bothered with the trivial pleasantries of talking about the weather.

Today would be my first time working directly with her and I wasn't sure what to expect as we walked into the room filled with Timbre employees.

The meeting began unceremoniously with Lola explaining in Spanish that we would be discussing the TSA's required for

Timbre in preparation for our meetings with the higher ups at Grupo Merced.

I sat at my seat, taking notes for George. He was glancing at my laptop occasionally, to see what I was sharing, but after a few moments he seemed to get distracted on his own computer. I glanced over and saw that he'd opened a browser page for Disney Cruise Lines and rolled my eyes.

I almost nudged him to pay attention, but Lola was handling the meeting so well, that it didn't seem necessary.

The Timbre employees looked pleased. Some of them were taking notes, others were just listening with focused faces and Lola was poised and calm. She was definitely in her element.

I clicked away from my notes for a moment to check my email inbox and started to read an email from my dad, when I heard Lola say the word, *beneficios.*

I stopped what I was doing, tuned into listen, and realized that Lola was now off script.

I pinged George with a message. "Are you tracking this conversation at all?"

He lifted his head with a quizzical look... "No, you know I don't speak Spanish," he typed back. "What's going on?"

I wrote him back, "Instead of Lola asking the team what processes and technology are in place today to run the business, she is asking them what they would like to have? The Timbre team is getting excited about the perks they could have from Grupo Merced."

George quickly skimmed my message and immediately chimed in and stopped the group dead in their tracks. "Are you all talking about the processes and technology that are required to continue to run the business?" he asked.

Lola darted her eyes in my direction. She knew I had alerted George to what was happening.

Efrian chimed in before Lola could cover her tracks. "No, we are talking about what we would like to have from the Grupo Merced team in advance of the transition."

George looked at Lola and then continued. "The intention of this conversation is to understand what is absolutely required to run the business. We do not want to ask Grupo Merced for anything additional. Anything new that isn't required will cause issues during our negotiations." George nodded at me in approval and then messaged me, "Thank you."

After finishing up the discussion with the group. Lola called for a lunch break and said we'd be doing a Q & A afterwards where Timbre employees could ask questions.

I walked out of the room feeling just as nervous as I'd felt when I walked in. I was glad I had clued George in, but I also couldn't help but feel a pit in my stomach as if I had betrayed what little trust Lola and I shared.

I walked toward the hallway to get some water when I heard Lola calling my name. I stopped in my tracks and turned on the spot.

"Hola, Lola," I said. She gave me a look that was impossible to misread.

"You didn't need to involve George. I was getting what we needed."

I could feel the lump in my throat. "I'm sorry," I said. "But it's my job to translate the meetings for the non-Spanish speakers and Jake and George made it clear how important it was to stick to the script."

"You heard me say follow my lead in there, didn't you?" she asked.

"I was only trying to help," I said.

"Next time, help less."

I nodded but felt my cheeks begin to burn. I held my hand up to my forehead. It felt hot. I wanted some air.

"Coffee?" Gio appeared at my side.

"Yes please," I replied.

We walked down to the lobby again and I didn't say much. My head was still reeling from the meeting.

"You're quiet," he said.

"Yeah..." I admitted. "I'm... that meeting was... Lola is just so. I dunno."

"She's not very friendly," he said.

"Not at all! And honestly, she snapped at me, and it felt awful."

"I'm sorry," he said sympathetically.

"That's OK," I said.

As we neared the coffee shop again, we saw Sam toward the doors and Gio's shoulders tensed.

"Gio," he called. "Deberías pensarlo." *You should think about it.* Then he exited out onto the street.

I looked up at Gio. He knew I understood what Sam said. I raised an eyebrow and his face looked resigned.

"Think about what?" I asked.

He looked caught. "It's nothing."

"Ahuh..." I gave him a look that I hoped conveyed playful doubt.

"Let's just say that the part of my past that relates to Sam is over. I'm happy in my new life, but this particular job is bringing me a bit closer to that old life than I would like." He looked directly into my eyes as he spoke, and my skepticism started to grow.

"You're not going to tell me anything more are you?"

"Not today," he said.

"Is everything okay?" I asked.

"Yes," he said. "Just swatting away flies."

CHAPTER SEVEN
Lola

"No matter what happens in these meetings, we must stick to the plan." Charles spoke as we all sat around the conference room table in our office preparing for the day's meetings. "We have to stay focused and work within the parameters of the deal." He wasn't looking at Lola, but we all knew he was talking to her.

I had been in the car when George had informed Jake and Charles what had happened during the meeting that Lola had run with the Timbre employees. Jake was livid, but Charles suggested that we not alienate our Mexico Team by reprimanding her.

"We need to be credible in our request," Jake now added. "Asking for anything that is not currently in place will make the Grupo Merced team think everything is up for negotiation."

"Right," George agreed. "These guys are going to be sharks and we need to make sure they can't see or sense any vulnerabilities on our end."

I glanced at Lola. She looked irritated. "Lo siento equipo. I was trying to help," she said. "Tomas is going to be tough. We will need negotiation leverage."

It was starting to hit me how big of a deal this merger really was. Billions of dollars had changed hands in this merger, and we had to get it right. I'd known this going in, but the stakes had begun to sink in more and more each day. An international merger wasn't Professor Patterson's business negations class, and with

Lola having gone rogue in the last meeting, I was worried that our team had lost some credibility with our client. I had concerns that we weren't as coordinated as we should be. It wasn't until I reached down to wipe my hands on my skirt that I realized my palms were sweating.

The entire team was nervous going into our first meeting with Grupo Merced and it was incredibly apparent as our cars neared the office location.

I had begun to recognize everyone's nervous tell. Jake's go to move was to be on his phone, George would begin to hum. Charles would sit very still and quiet, in an almost meditative state. Max picked his cuticles, Ricardo's forehead would have a slight shine to it, Chela looked a bit nauseous, Lola's brow would furrow deeply, and her eyes would narrow in the most spectacular display of resting bitch face I'd ever seen. And for me it was sweaty palms. I wiped my hands on my skirt and took a deep breath. George was still humming in the back seat.

I knew by reputation that the guys at the top of Grupo Merced were going to be tough, and no matter how prepared we were, it was impossible not to feel the tension.

As we piled out of the car, I looked at Ricardo, "Is Tomas really in a cartel?"

He looked at me concerned, "Not now, Blake."

I had the distinct feeling that a lot of people were keeping some pivotal information from me, and I didn't like it. Were we involved in a business deal with a cartel boss?

Arriving at Tomas Barajas' office was like being transported into a completely different world than the places we'd visited since arriving in Mexico City. The security was extensive. Body scanners, bag scanners, pat downs, IDs left at the front desk. It was tighter than any airport security I'd ever experienced. I wondered if that was a move to make us feel unsettled and throw us off our game a little bit, or if Grupo Merced had reason to be discerning with who entered their office complex.

I watched Gio go through the security with us, and the security guards seemed to recognize him. My intuition started perking up again. There was something in the way they scrutinized him that made me feel slightly protective of him, even though I knew he was more than capable of taking care of himself.

"Ven conmigo por favor," said a man, who looked like a bouncer, as he led us down a long corridor. I glanced around at my team members as we walked, George was humming quietly, Jake was checking his phone again, Ricardo and Chela followed closely behind Lola as if she was the mother duck.

Gio was the only one walking confidently down the hallway as if he owned the place. It was hot and for a moment I was distracted from my own nervous, clammy hands.

Eventually the corridor ended, and we were outside again. We had been dropped in a beautiful, lush garden that surrounded a large driveway. Sitting in the driveway were numerous SUVs and sports cars. My breath caught in my chest at the sight of it. It was beyond my imagination. It was impossible to believe that we were still in Mexico City, let alone in an office complex.

Max looked at me. "You feeling like we just got transported halfway around the world? Or just me?" The bouncer guy turned his head sharply and Max instantly looked down at his shoes. We were led over a beautiful wooden bridge and over the most stunning koi pond, eventually leading us into the office.

Once inside, we were brought into the conference room and sat around a large table.

"Wait here," the bouncer guy said, and then he left the room.

We took our seats. It was dead quiet except for George's nervous humming. After a short while, Efrain and the Timbre team arrived and were seated in the same room as us. There were refreshments on the table, but no one reached for them. I scanned the room looking for Gio, but noticed he was waiting outside in an atrium. Having him farther away made me even more nervous. We sat there in silence waiting. I wanted nothing more than to talk with my team, to ease the tension, but no one dared speak. I watched them checking their phones, shuffling papers around again, checking details on their computers. Eventually even George stopped humming. The tension was high.

After almost thirty minutes Tomas and his team arrived. As he walked into the room my heart picked up pace and started hammering against my ribs. Tomas was a scary looking man. He was burly – at least six foot five. He had scars on his face and humongous hands that looked like he could smoosh me like a bug.

He and his team sat down at the table, and they exchanged a few hellos with some of the people they recognized. A woman walked over and gave Tomas a steaming cup of coffee then she leaned down and said in a low voice, "tú hermano llamo por teléfono." *Your brother called.*

Tomas waived her away like he was swatting at a fly. Then he took a sip of his coffee and then exhaled, audibly. "Well, what are we waiting for?" he asked.

I had to fight the urge to roll my eyes.

"Thank you for having us today," Jake said, and he then began the meeting in Spanish.

I sat at my computer, diligently taking notes to translate for George, Charles, and Max. I felt self-conscious hearing the keyboard clicks of my laptop. The room was so quiet you could have heard a pin drop and I felt like the sound of my typing was bouncing off the walls. No one else seemed to notice however and Jake was poised and was leading the negation with a deft hand.

At first, I thought that maybe we had overestimated Grupo Merced. Tomas was listening intently and nodding as Jake brought up certain terms of the sale. I started to feel a sense of relief, that maybe we'd sail right through this meeting and into a nice team dinner. Maybe Gio would join us, and I would get to learn more about him and his interests...

"No!" Tomas' deep voice interrupted my reverie. I snapped back to attention. "¡Eso no es possible!"

I looked over at my team and thought I heard Max gulp audibly.

"I'm sorry?" Jake said, trying to toe the line.

Tomas took a sip of his coffee, cleared his voice, and then spoke in English, which somehow made him seem more menacing. "We do not agree to support Timbre and we will not be agreeing to any of your TSAs."

At this point Efrain started to speak in Spanish. "Tomas, these TSAs are not required long term. However, we still need Grupo Merced's support in the short term. It was your decision to sell the Timbre division. What can we do without these basic needs met?"

"Grupo Merced will not and cannot support Timbre any longer," Tomas said again. His tone was firm. It was clear there would be no arguing with him.

There was a deafening silence around the table again. Where could we go from here? We were out of moves. We simply had not anticipated that Grupo Merced would outright refuse a transitional period during the merger.

"Señor Barajas," Jake began. "We really need to continue this discussion..." There was a pleading quality to his voice. I closed my eyes with resignation. What if he said no?

"I think you will." I heard Lola's voice and opened my eyes.

"Excuse me?" Tomas' eyes narrowed as he questioned her.

"I think you will support Timbre," she said firmly. "Transitional Service Agreements are standard with any merger. You know this, Tomas. You've been in business for decades. Grupo Merced cannot just flip a switch and be done with Timbre. There are legal ramifications if you choose to do that."

I looked at Tomas. He looked livid. I was expecting at any moment to see his hair burst into flame. I watched as he interlaced his fingers and then his lips curled up into a condescending smile. "What are you suggesting?"

"Only the status quo," Lola said. "We will help you in identifying where your team is spending their time and where you are still intertwined with the division you have sold off. Once we identify those areas, we will determine an exit strategy for the Timbre and Grupo Merced team. We will be happy to discuss more details with you at any time."

"No quiero hablar contigo." Tomas uttered, teeth clenched.

"Well, I don't want to be speaking with you either, Señor Barajas, but nevertheless, here we are... speaking."

I heard a gasp in the back of the room.

I looked at Lola and my heart swelled. She was kicking so much ass. It began to hit me why she had gone off script before. Lola knew Tomas. Or she knew men like him, and she knew how to get what she wanted from them. I made a note to never underestimate her again.

"The purpose of this meeting—" Tomas began.

"The purpose of this meeting is now a lost cause," Lola said evenly. "So, allow me to simplify this for you. You will agree to the transitional service agreements for the Timbre division that you sold off. If you cannot do that, our client will have no choice but to file a lawsuit against Grupo Merced and I'm guessing that getting entangled with American lawyers wouldn't work well for you and your... other business endeavors. No?"

Tomas looked like he was about to explode. He narrowed his eyes. "Ten cuidado, niña." *Be careful, little girl.*

I looked at Lola, but she didn't flinch.

At that point Jake cleared his throat and spoke. "Should we break for lunch?"

"No," Tomas said. "We are done here." He stood up from his chair and walked swiftly out of the room. As he passed Gio I saw him pause and gesture toward him. Gio nodded calmly. I didn't like Tomas being so close to him. I still had so many unanswered questions.

The rest of the Grupo Merced team filed out of the room after Tomas and then the bouncer guy was back to escort us out.

As Gio walked into the conference room he made eye contact with me. "You okay?" he mouthed to me. I nodded.

"Are you?" I mouthed back. He nodded.

As we walked out, I walked more quickly to catch up to Lola. I touched her wrist and she looked up at me.

"You were amazing in there," I whispered to her. "Truly! I'm so sorry about before."

"It's okay," she whispered back to me. Then she took my hand and gave it a small squeeze.

CHAPTER EIGHT
Bailamos

Charles raised his glass. "To well-deserved drinks after a tough day!"

"Cheers!" We all exclaimed as we raised our glasses.

Drinks at Porfirio's were definitely necessary after our confrontation with Tomas. While none of us were sure how Grupo Merced would react after today's meeting, we were very sure that we'd conveyed the strength of our team and defended our client, and that seemed like something to drink to.

"I will admit, I wasn't sure how we were going to move forward if Tomas didn't agree to the TSA's," Jake said.

"Si, pero Lola fue muy fuerte!" Chela added. *Yes, but Lola was strong.*

We all laughed. I looked to Gio, and he seemed pensive. He wasn't engaging in the laughter at Tomas' expense. Once again it gave me pause. Gio seemed to have unique insights into Grupo Merced, and I wasn't sure if we were fully understanding. He must have noticed me studying his face because he pivoted his expression into a smile and shrugged his shoulders at me.

"What's the matter Blake? Es una fiesta!" He raised his glass. "To standing up to rude men o hombres groseros!"

Everyone cheered.

Charles ordered every appetizer on the menu for all of us to share and as the night rolled on, I began to forget that we might have pissed off a drug lord. There were tacos, elote, ceviche, and so many margaritas. Chela and Ricardo were glowing, feeling very proud of what their boss, or *jefa* as Ricardo endearingly called her, had accomplished today. Even George seemed to relax after the mishap from the days before and he and Lola shared a few smiles.

I sipped my margarita slowly, savoring the tang of the lime and salt and the feel of the cold ice cubes against my lips. Gio stood up from the table to take a call, but before he walked outside, he smiled at me, and I felt my stomach tighten. I couldn't quite place the feeling. It wasn't nerves, it was more like longing. *Oh man, Blake. What are you getting yourself into?* I took a deep breath and tried to get my head straight, but I couldn't help it as my cheeks yanked my lips into a goofy grin.

"Blake." Lola appeared at my side. "Ricardo, give me your chair for a moment. Girl talk." Ricardo grumbled something but eventually switched seats with Lola.

"Hi Lola," I said. For a moment I was worried I'd done something wrong, but then she took my hand.

"I want to apologize for the way I talked to you the other day," she said. "I realize that I'm so used to working with all these machismo men that I sometimes... how do you say? Come off a little bit too strong."

"Oh, Lola it's okay—"

"Other than Chela, and my mother and sister I don't spend a lot of time with women," she continued. "I don't have a lot of amigas in my life. From what I've been seeing you are doing a great job here. You're very smart and hardworking, and I think we got off on the wrong foot. I'd like for us to be friends."

"I'd like that too," I said.

"Bueno," she said.

"Si, bueno," I replied.

Lola reached for her drink, clinked glasses with mine and took a sip. I did the same.

Gio walked back inside and the second our eyes met, he smiled at me again. I felt my cheeks flush.

"This man only smiles when you're around," Lola said. I closed my eyes and sighed, trying to signal to her not to make a big deal out of it, but she just laughed lightly and stood up. "Gio, you can take my seat. I'm going to the bar."

"Gracias, Lola," Gio said as he sat down next to me.

"Blake," Ricardo called to me from across the table. "Are you enjoying your time here in Mexico City?"

"I am!"

"What's on your list of things you want to see?"

I thought for a moment. I'd gotten to do and see so many things already, but I really wanted to go Salsa dancing. "Going to Salsa is on the top of my Mexico City bucket list!"

"Well, we should go then!" Chela chimed in animatedly.

"Totally!" I agreed.

"No, I mean ahora! Now, silly!" she said.

I thought she was joking with me. "You really know somewhere we could go on a Tuesday?"

"¡Claro que sí! We're in Mexico City."

We arrived at Mama Rumba around nine o'clock. I was thrilled to learn that they did a salsa class before the club really took off. George, Charles, and Jake had called it a night already, so our group consisted of, Chela, Lola, Ricardo, Max, Gio and me.

As we walked in, we were still some of the first people in the club, which made it feel empty given the sheer size of the club! The first floor had multiple bars with a huge stage at the center and the upper floor had a balcony around the entire room and additional dance floors and bars above. The music was already playing and the energy in the room excited me.

I felt eager to brush up on my skills since I hadn't danced salsa since high school. I was equal parts thrilled and nervous to make a fool out of myself, but the tequila was making me brave.

We began with the instructor reminding us of the steps. We'd step in place, one-two-three, then step forward, one-two-three, backward; one-two-three, to the side; one-two-three, to the other side.

Max was paired with me, and we both laughed as we worked out the steps together. He was very much a beginner, but he was totally game to try something new and experience the culture in the name of having fun. I tried to guide him, but the teacher came over and gently scolded me and told me to let him lead.

"Gender norms!" I joked to Max.

"I'm happy to be the follower if it means I can move my feet the right way," he said playfully.

"Now, hombres in a big outer circle," said the teacher. "And mujeres in an inner circle facing the men."

We filed into conjoining circles and when we stopped, Gio was right in front of me. He smiled his devilish smile, and I couldn't help but melt a little bit at the sight of him.

The music began and the rhythms filled the club. I looked up at him, expecting him to lead. He seemed unsure if he could touch me, but further emboldened by the drinks, I grabbed his hand and away we went.

Gio was a great dance partner, I felt our bodies sync up immediately as he gently guided me around the floor. There was something undeniably sexy about watching our hips move in tandem, even if we weren't particularly close physically. I could have danced with Gio all night, but at some point, it was time to switch partners and he twirled me over to Ricardo.

"Is this what you were hoping for?" Ricardo asked me loudly over the music. He was clumsier in his step, but he made up for it with his enthusiasm.

"Yes!" I replied as we circled the floor.

Next, I danced with Max who was finally getting the hang of the steps and showed off a little bit with his new-found moves.

"Okay!" I called to him. "You got this!"

"I'm trying, girl!" he said.

After that I got lost in the rhythm, I was dancing with a series of people on the floor that I didn't know. They seemed to be locals and they were all very skilled in their dancing. As my partner twirled me around the dance floor my whole body relaxed, and my cheeks were starting to hurt from laughing and smiling. I was so lost in the music that I thought I heard someone call my name.

"Blake!" There it was again.

Eventually I looked up and saw Gio near the wall of the club. He was gesturing for me to come over to where he was.

"Excuse me," I said to the man I was dancing with, and I made my way over. Gio grinned at me, and I grinned right back. I was having a great night. "What's up?"

"You know, you really should stay with the group," he said playfully. "It's protocol."

"Oh, really?" I teased him. "Are you not liking watching me dance with these other men?"

"Oh, no it's just for your safety," he continued with mock-sincerity.

"Tell me more." I matched his tone. *Oh my god! Are we flirting?!*

"Well, you are a beautiful woman..."

"A huh..."

"And any sort of bad guy could come in and just..."

"Steal me away?"

"Si! Yes.... So, ya know, for your own safety, you should probably just dance with me tonight. If you like..."

"Well, I guess I have no choice then. Shall we?" I took his hand and led him back onto the dance floor.

We returned to the hotel well after midnight. Gio walked Max and I into the lobby to say goodnight, but Max scurried away to the elevator with barely a word. I wondered if he also had noticed the connection with Gio and me and didn't want to interrupt.

"That was really fun," I said.

"I'm glad Chela suggested it," he agreed.

"Me too." I was sure I should walk toward the elevator and call it a night, but something had me rooted on the spot. I looked up at Gio and as our eyes locked, I felt that feeling of longing again.

For a moment it looked like he was going to say something, but he just smiled at me kind of awkwardly. "Would you like me to walk you to your room?" he asked.

"Alright," I agreed.

We walked toward the elevator in silence. His arm was very close to mine and again I could feel my entire body buzzing at the nearness of him.

We stood in the elevator as the doors closed and I was very aware of the sound of both of our breathing. When we approached my hotel room door, I noticed that my heart rate started to increase. *Was he going to come in? Was something going to happen?*

We arrived at my room, and I turned to face him. "Gracias," I said.

"De nada," he replied.

I reached up to hug him and as he put his arms around my waist, he nearly lifted me off the floor. On my tip toes, I rested into his embrace, my head against his chest. He felt strong and I felt safe. For a moment neither of us said anything, we just held each other. Then he leaned down and placed a kiss on my forehead before resting his forehead against mine. We stood there, barely moving, our noses rested gently against each other. It was electrifying. His scent was intoxicating. I didn't want to move. For an instant I was terrified that I was being horribly unprofessional, but I tipped my face up slightly, so my lips just barely caught his bottom lip in the most miniscule of kisses.

To my complete and utter joy, he pressed his lips into mine, returning the kiss. When he pulled his face away, he was smiling the most adorably sheepish smile.

"Buenas noches, Bella," *Goodnight beautiful.*

"Good night." I could feel my smile stretch from ear to ear. When I closed the door to my room, I squealed like a 16-year-old girl. He probably heard me, but I didn't care. I pulled out my phone and had a text from Mia.

"How are you doing?!" it read.

I replied immediately. "I'll call you tomorrow. I have news! And it involves *passión*!"

I was floating as I got myself ready for bed. I have no idea how long I laid in my bed smiling to myself, unable to sleep, thinking about him, but at some point, my reality blended with my dreams and the whole night became about Gio.

CHAPTER NINE
Más Problemas

I exited the shower the next morning and noticed that my hands were shaking. I knew it was mostly because I was hungover, but it was also because I would be seeing Gio as soon as I went downstairs. I was excited to see him, but also nervous, and then there was the added pressure of needing to play it extra cool, so my colleagues didn't suspect that we'd kissed.

I closed my eyes and let my mind recall the moment. The way he'd smelled, the way his lips felt against mine. Good first kisses were magical and this one was no exception.

"Hoo boy." I then took a deep breath and exhaled, hoping that would calm me down, but when I looked back at my hands, they were still shaking. "Well, this should be interesting."

As I got dressed, I felt like I still smelled of tequila, limes, and salt. My stomach turned a little bit at the thought. My head was pounding, and I said a silent prayer as I took two Advil with a glass of water. I was glad to know that today's workday would be a bit lighter, and I could relax a bit while I waited to return to feeling normal. Charles had sent an email late last night telling us all to come in around 10:00AM since he knew we had all been out late together. We were embracing the Mexican way.

I was the last to arrive down to the lobby. As I walked toward our group, I tried not to look at Gio right away, but he drew my eyes to him like a magnet.

"Coffee?" he asked, holding out a cup to me. I looked up and noticed that everyone else had matching cups and he was carrying a cardboard tray from the coffee place. He had arrived with coffee for the team, and I was touched by his thoughtfulness.

"Oh, you are my hero," I blurted out without thinking. Gio's face froze, and he suddenly looked self-conscious. I glanced around, worried that I'd blown our cover, but everyone else was busy staring at their phones, checking emails. "Umm... I mean... thank you for the coffee." I tried to sound casual.

"You're welcome," he replied curtly.

My heart seized in my chest, and for a moment I panicked thinking that he regretted what had happened. I stared down at my phone trying to hide the series of worried thoughts that were flying through my brain. *Was I a bad kisser? Did I do something wrong? Was he dating someone else?*

"Blake, you look pretty rough," George's voice pulled me out of my reverie. "Did you enjoy your big night out?"

"I did," I replied, trying to force some enthusiasm. "A little bit too much."

"Cars are here," Jake said, and we headed out for the day.

Even arriving at the office at ten o'clock, it was still virtually empty, and for once I felt relieved for the more casual Mexico City start time. It was around noon before Lola filed in and nearly twelve-thirty before Chela and Ricardo followed suit.

Jake, George, and Charles were working hard preparing materials for an upcoming meeting with Carlos and they had me formatting and finalizing slides for the meeting.

"Do you think we're at risk based on the last meeting?" I asked. "Grupo Merced doesn't really seem like they'll budge."

"We're not sure yet," Charles said. "Lola's standing up to Tomas seems to have worked in our favor. His team asked me to email them the TSA terms. For now, let's just let Carlos know that we're on watch and we'll put mitigating actions in place to ensure no major risks become issues."

"Okay," I agreed and added a bit more information to the slides before sending the files to them. I was starving and ready for lunch at La Califa. "Should we break for lunch soon?" I asked.

"Huh?" Jake looked up from his computer confused.

"It's almost one," I said. "Should we break for lunch? Califa?"

"We've got too much to prep for this Carlos meeting," Charles answered.

"Oh," I responded, feeling disappointed.

"But why don't you and Gio go and pick up tacos for the team?" he suggested.

"Sure," I said, pulling out a pad and pen. "What does everyone want?" I took down their orders and grabbed my bag from my chair.

Right on cue, Gio appeared in the conference room ready to go with me. "Ready?" he asked.

I nodded.

We walked to the elevator in silence and suddenly, I felt self-conscious. It started to hit me that I'd definitely mixed business with pleasure and then I started thinking about what it would be like if things were weird with Gio for the rest of my time here. What if he was angry with me? What if I had ruined this? The idea that things between us would be awkward or that he was upset made me feel sick to my stomach. We exited the building into the sunshine.

"Pretty day," I said, trying desperately to ease the tension I felt.

"It is," he agreed. "How was your head this morning?"

"What?" I asked, unsure what he meant. *Was he wanting to talk about how I felt?*

"Do you have a headache?" he asked, chuckling. "You enjoyed muchas margaritas last night, Chica."

"Oh," I responded, understanding. "My head has been better! But I think the food will help."

"I'm sure it will."

"I think that maybe it would be a good idea for—owe!" The heel of my shoe suddenly caught in a crack in the sidewalk, and I tripped. *Oh no...* I thought as I started to topple, but Gio's reflexes were lightning-quick, and he caught me before I hit the ground.

"Are you okay?" he asked, as he steadied me. "Let me see your ankle."

We sat down on the curb, and he looked at my foot. I reached for my shoe, which was still stuck in the crack in the sidewalk.

"I'm okay, don't worry," I said.

I felt his fingers caress my skin as he examined my ankle. "Can you bend it?" he asked.

"Yes," I said softly, matching his tender tone. I wiggled my ankle. It felt okay. I looked up into his eyes. They were warm and I felt calm. "Are we going to talk about last night? Or pretend nothing happened?"

He laughed. "We can talk about it, but not here. Let me take you to dinner."

"Dinner? When?" I asked maybe a little too excited.

He chuckled. "I was thinking tomorrow after work."

"So, like a date?" I asked, wondering if I'd heard him correctly.

"Yes," he answered. "Like a date."

"What about the others?" I asked.

"It's not really their business, is it?" He had a mischievous grin spread across his face and it excited me.

"No," I agreed. "No es el asunto de ellos."

We returned to the office with everyone's food and a plan of our own. We would meet tomorrow night at eight o'clock. If anyone asked, I'd tell them that I wanted to spend the evening in with room service to finish up some work. I wasn't sure where we were going or what would happen, but I was more excited than I was willing to admit to myself.

"Blake, we need you." Jake's voice brought me back to reality before I'd even finished my lunch, or my daydream. "I want you to come with us to the Carlos meeting?"

"Okay," I agreed, my mouth full of food.

He walked over to where I was sitting. "Can you take notes and share screen with the team during the meeting?" he asked.

I took a sip of water and swallowed my food. "Yes, of course."

"Great, we're leaving in five."

So much for a chill day. I had barely swallowed my last bite of carne asada when we were on our way back out the door.

Despite the way the day began, I was feeling great. My headache had faded after eating and I was giddy about my pending date with Gio. *A date!* Walking out the door, I was pleased to be included in such an important meeting.

Carlos was in the conference room, finishing up a phone call when we entered the Timbre offices. He waved us in as he wrapped up his conversation.

We exchanged pleasantries with him and then collected our materials to discuss with him. I sat down and opened my laptop, prepared to start taking notes as soon as the meeting began.

"How are you guys?" Carlos asked. "I heard there was some salsa dancing last night." He looked to me, some levity behind his eyes.

"News travels fast around here," I said.

"I'm glad the city is treating you all well!" he laughed.

Jake got down to brass tax. "So, Carlos, we wanted to update you on the meetings with Grupo Merced, the current risks we foresee, and also team morale across the Timbre, Grupo Merced and Global Core teams."

"Great," Carlos chimed in. "On the team morale side, I'd like to understand how Efrain is doing and also talk about the incident with your team and Grupo Merced."

Jake looked surprised. "The incident?"

"I heard there was some tension between your team and Tomas," he said.

"Wow, news really *does* travel fast around here," Jake marveled. "Alright then let's start with the discussions about Timbre and Grupo Merced."

George began. "Things are going well. The Timbre team is giving us everything we need to identify their needs to continue running the business successfully until we can fully transition them over to PacSouth."

"So much so that Grupo Merced wasn't pleased with our requests regarding the TSAs and Lola laid down the hammer. As I assume you heard," Jake said. "Tomas left that meeting feeling less than pleased, but I think he understands the need for TSAs and is aligned to moving forward. We are going to get the Timbre team what they need."

"Jake..." Carlos sounded thoughtful. "Your team needs to be careful. You don't know what Grupo Merced, specifically Tomas is capable of. I appreciate that you are all doing what is right for our business, but I want to ensure you are doing what is also right for your people."

At this, I paused my note taking. *What did he mean by 'what they are capable of'?*

The room quieted down pretty quickly. I glanced at my team, and everyone seemed to be stunned.

"Understood," Jake said with forced calm. "We're being careful. The security detail has made us all feel much safer, right guys? We don't go anywhere without our guy."

"Good," said Carlos. "I think that's best. This deal is going to be more tense than anyone of us realized."

I sat there, rooted to the spot, staring at Carlos, trying to fully process what he was saying. There was always a part of me that knew that Mexico could be dangerous, but I never thought I'd encounter that dark underbelly. I had been so hell-bent on coming here and telling my family and friends back home that Mexico City was perfectly safe. I hadn't wanted to see that there might be more to it than met the eye. And now as I heard Carlos warning Jake to be cautious, for the first time since Gio arrived, I felt worried.

"One of the biggest risks we foresee has to do with the network towers," Jake said. "Ricardo has been looking into our options there, but it appears that they are located on land that may or may not belong to one of the cartels."

"I will speak with Ricardo about this separately," Carlos said.

As they continued the meeting, I took notes, but I was barely registering what they said. I started wondering how me, a twenty-two-year-old recent college graduate had ended up on a project this big and this dangerous. Was it because Jake had faith in me? Was it because I was bilingual? Was it because no one else wanted the gig? Here Carlos had told the team that was supposed to be negotiating for his company, not to push too hard, and to be careful. He was acting against his own interest, and it surprised me. I needed to know the truth of what I was dealing with. Did my family have just cause to be worried for my safety? I needed to get some answers about Tomas and Grupo Merced, and if Gio didn't want to tell me then I'd have to ask my Mexican colleagues.

CHAPTER TEN
La Cita Romántica

When I got back to the hotel that evening, I made the decision to skip dinner with the team and go for a run instead.

"Are you alright?" Gio asked me.

"Just need to clear my head," I offered. "I'll see you tomorrow."

I went to my room to get changed for the gym. I just wanted to run on the treadmill and try and release some of the anxiety I had been feeling. As I walked into the W's gym, I saw my colleagues crossing the street to head out to dinner and I was thankful to have some time to myself. I had been with them for what felt like, every night for weeks and after the events of the day I just needed to do something other than drinking and talking.

I put my earbuds in and began jogging at moderate pace. As soon as I started to break a sweat, the endorphins began to flow, and I felt some relief.

There was so much to consider. There was the meeting with Carlos and his warning; there was the situation with Gio. Here we were planning to sneak off tomorrow for a date and I still had not made up my mind if mixing business and pleasure was a good idea. I had sent a few emails to my parents since I'd arrived, but I knew I owed them a phone call and now that we had security detail, I was kind of dreading talking to them because I knew I'd have to omit the truth. I started to pick up the pace to try and push the anxiety out of my body. I turned up the volume of the music to try and block out my thoughts and I just focused on putting one foot in front of the other.

After I ran for a half an hour, I moved over to the weight station and decided to bite the bullet and call my parents. There was no one else in the gym, so I figured I wasn't breaking any kind of rules, disturbing other guests. I sat on one of the benches and dialed their number. My heartrate quickened even more with every ring of the phone. As luck would have it, the machine picked up. They must have been out. I left a message.

"Hi guys, it's me. Hola!" I said awkwardly. "I know we haven't really spoken much since I got here and I'm actually not supposed to use my minutes much, but I wanted to let you know that everything is good here. I really miss you guys, but I'm having a great time and learning a lot. Send me an email when you can and maybe we can figure out a time for a FaceTime call soon. Okay love you! Bye."

I hung up. Relieved, feeling like I'd done my duty as a good daughter, and a little nauseous that I'd lied and told them everything was fine. But everything was fine. I tried to convince myself.

After my workout, I returned to my room, took a shower, and poured myself a glass of wine. As I sipped it down, I felt myself relax. I dried my hair and laid out my clothes for the next day and then I jumped on a FaceTime call with Mia.

Seeing her face was surreal. I hadn't seen anyone but my team in weeks. As I saw her smiling at me, I felt a tug in my gut, and I realized that I'd been so busy I hadn't even taken the time to let myself feel even the slightest bit homesick.

"Hi!" she exclaimed as we made the connection. "Oh my god! Is that your room!?"

I laughed. "Can you believe it? Insane, right?"

"You have stairs!"

I started to feel more like myself, just seeing her face and hearing her voice. "I do!"

I filled her in on the PG-rated version of what had happened since I arrived. The merger, the situation with the taxi and then Gio. I left out the part about Carlos' warning and the voicemail I'd left for my folks.

"So is Gio the guy you texted me about last night?" Mia asked. "You mentioned *passión*!"

I laughed. "Well... we did kiss."

"WHAT!?"

"I have so many emotions about it!" I squealed. "He's so hot and we have a date tomorrow."

"Oh my god, Blake! You should have packed that red dress!"

"I know, I know! You were right."

"That's all I needed to hear. So, what's it like having a security guard?"

"There's kind of a downside," I lamented. "I can't go anywhere on my own, not even to the corner store for toothpaste!"

"Are you out of toothpaste?" She teased me. "I think the concierge can get you some more!"

I laughed. "I just mean as an example."

"I get it," she agreed. "I can see how that would make you feel like a kid back in middle school. Is he outside your door now?"

"No, it's not like that. He just escorts us back to our hotel at night."

"I see," she said. "Well at least he's hot."

I laughed. "True. He's very nice to look at."

"How's everything else?"

"It's good! But there are little things that I didn't think about that I'm now getting used to. I can't even brush my teeth with the water in the sink!" I continued. "I guess I hadn't realized how much I was still adjusting. "I have to be careful not to accidentally drink the water when I shower or end up with Montezuma's revenge. It's been an adjustment, ya know? And it's things like that that have been the hardest. The things I took for granted at home that I now miss."

"And me, of course," she said laughing, her face softening. "Are you enjoying it, though? This is what you wanted, right? You're living abroad; you're using your Spanish speaking abilities in a business setting and my gosh—the cherry on top! A hot guy who's into you!? I'm honestly jealous."

I took a deep breath. *She was right.* "You're right," I allowed. "You're totally right. There's a lot going right. I think I'm just tired."

"It makes sense! You're working hard!"

"Yes, I am," I said, feeling grateful.

"Well, I can't wait to hear about your date!" she squealed. "Text me updates!"

"Okay," I said through a yawn.

"I'll let you go," she said. "Love you!"

"Love you!"

I put the computer down beside me and closed my eyes. When I opened them again, it was almost midnight and I realized I had fallen asleep. The warm glow of my computer screensaver illuminated the room. The curtains were still open, and the sparkling lights of the city shone out my window. I walked over to the window and peered out. My life had changed so much in just a couple months. It was starting to feel serious. Like I was an actual adult, and there was no going back.

Mia was right that I should try to focus on the positives. There were so many things going right.

I reached for my phone on the bed and saw a text from Gio. "We missed you at dinner tonight."

I responded. "Still on for tomorrow night?"

It was only a moment before he replied. "Yes." I smiled to myself as I climbed under the sheets to sleep.

Work was tense the next day, and not just because I was counting the hours until my date with Gio. I could tell that Jake was trying to play it cool, but he seemed a little bit shaken by our meeting with Carlos. He had several quiet conversations with George and Charles throughout the day. I tried to keep my head down and push things forward.

"What do you think they're talking about?" Chela asked me.

"I'm not sure, but I think it has to do with Tomas."

"Ay dios mio," she said. "He makes me muy nerviosa."

"He's definitely a scary guy," I agreed. "Carlos told Jake that it was more important to keep our team safe than to push too hard for the Timbre team."

Chela looked at me surprised. "That's not a good sign."

Ricardo leaned into our conversation, "Blake, I need to talk to you about Tomas."

"Okay..." I said.

Ricardo moved his seat closer to Chela and me and lowered his voice. "The history of Mexico is a complicated one..."

"Wait... You're giving me a history lesson?" I teased.

"Just wait," he said. "It's worth knowing."

"Okay."

"Are you aware of *la Guerra contra el narcotraficante?*"

"Si," I nodded. I had studied the history of Mexico in some of my Spanish classes at SMU.

"Then you must be familiar with the name Miguel Ángel Felix Gallardo."

"I am," I agreed. "He was the leader of the first Mexican drug cartel."

"Correct," he said. "He would oversee the distribution of cocaine from Colombia for Pablo Escobar's Medellin Cartel and the Cali Cartel. This took place for years. But Felix was arrested in 1989 and then the cartel in Mexico broke up into many different groups which included the Sinaloa Cartel, Juarez Cartel, Tajuana Cartel and Sonora Cartel."

"There has always been a rumor that Tomas' hermano is a high-ranking official a part of the Sinaloa cartel. Lola mentioned it when we first talked about him in our briefing. I, myself never believed it, but recently I talked to my brother about it, and he has more knowledge on the subject than I do. He believes that this is true, and that Grupo Merced does more than sell television shows and have a soccer team."

"Hang on a minute!" Max's voice startled me. I hadn't realized he was listening in too. "So, you think Grupo Merced is a front for the business the cartel is doing?"

Ricardo leaned in and quieted his voice. "I didn't fully believe it until I talked to my own brother. But now, I believe the telecom business was getting in the way of their most profitable business, so they decided to sell it. The faster the better."

"Ah, shi—"

"Hang on," I interrupted Max. "I'm still not clear. Are you saying Tomas is *part* of the cartel? Or that it's his brother?"

"No one knows for sure," Ricardo said. "But even if he is, he'd be careful to keep his hands clean and let's others do his bidding for him."

"Like Sam?" I whispered concerned.

"Like Sam." Ricardo finished. "And maybe a while ago... Gio."

I felt like I had been punched in the stomach. Suddenly it all made sense to me. The reason Sam kept contacting Gio and asking him to *think about things.* Gio had also been one of Tomas' right-hand men. I felt confused. He had told me that his old life was over and that he was happy, but was that the kind of past you could ever get away from?

The rest of the day passed in a blur. I had walked into the office so excited for my evening with Gio and now I wasn't even sure if I should go. I decided I'd at least give myself some time to think about my options so when we returned to the hotel that evening, I once again told the team I wanted to just workout and order room service.

"You okay?" Max asked me, concerned. "I know Ricardo brought up some pretty intense stuff today."

"I'm good," I replied, a bit too enthusiastically. "It's just been a long week and I should catch up with my parents."

"I think I'll do a chill night in tonight as well," Jake chimed in. "Gio, you can probably call it an early night if you want, unless anyone else needs him?"

"I'll eat in the hotel tonight," George said. "You guys wanna join me?"

"Sounds good!" Max and Charles agreed and just like that Gio was off the hook.

"I will see you guys tomorrow," Gio said. Then he looked at me and I saw the hint of that devilish smile pulling at the side of his mouth. My earlier worries started to fade.

"Well, goodnight guys," I said. "See y'all tomorrow." I rode the elevator up with Jake and then practically ran to my room to get ready. I took a lightning-fast shower, and then ran to my closet to try and find something presentable for a date.

Mia had been right. I should have packed a few sexier items. I truly had planned on being in business and casual attire during my time in Mexico City. I had no idea I'd meet someone while I was here and now, I was cursing myself that there wasn't anything remotely date-like in my closet.

"Great job, Blake," I lamented to myself. "Now what?" I thumbed through a few things in my drawer and discovered that I did have a black tee shirt that wasn't half bad. I found a pair of scissors in the desk drawer and carefully cut a bit off the length, so it was more of a cropped tee. Then I paired it with dark jeans, ankle boots and a long necklace. I curled my hair a bit and did my best to create a smokey eye. When all was said and done, I felt pretty satisfied.

I texted Gio. "Ready when you are."

"Meet me in the hotel bar and we'll head out," he wrote back

My heart was beating fast as I walked to the elevator and rode it down to the lobby. I was careful to hide my face as I passed the restaurant just in case Max, Charles, and George spotted me. I took a deep breath as I walked into the hotel bar. There was Gio standing there waiting for me. He had changed into a V-neck tee, blazer, and jeans. He looked casual and "off duty" that I almost didn't recognize him. He looked relaxed. It was sexy.

"Hi," I said. "You look so different! But great!"

He laughed. "You look great too." He took a moment and swallowed nervously. "Wow."

He leaned down to kiss me on the cheek.

"Thanks!" I felt my cheeks go red. "Where are we going?"

"You'll see," he said with a smirk. He grabbed me by the hand and whisked me out the door.

We ended up at a place called La No. 20 a few blocks down from the hotel. It was tucked away down a dimly lit alley. From the main street you'd never know it was there, but there it was. Leave it to Gio to take me to a hidden gem, that I'd never have known about otherwise.

The interior had a loungey kind of vibe and it seemed to be the kind of place where the who's who of Mexico City dined. The interiors were dark, and the ceiling was lit by hundreds of twinkling LED lights. In the middle of the room was the bar with a lit pyramid-style shelf that housed all the liquor bottles. It was impressive.

We approached the hostess stand.

"Gio," she cooed. "¡Buenas noches! Estás de Vuelta." It was clear she knew him. I wondered how well.

"Hola Juanita," he said. "¿Como estás?"

She sat us at a table tucked into a corner where we could have total privacy. Then she turned to me. "Enjoy." *Was that a wink?*

"Gracias," I said.

The table had a booth on one side and rather than sit in the chair across from me Gio scooted into the booth and sat next to me. It felt good to be close to him.

He picked up the wine list. "How do you feel about wine?" he asked. "I know we've consumed a lot of margaritas lately."

"Wine sounds really nice," I agreed. I was a little tequila'd out.

"This one is a red that's grown in the Valle de Guadalupe up north. Would you like to try that?"

"Sure!" I really liked being with someone so knowledgeable about the region. It made me feel like I had my own personal tour guide.

"How do you feel about food? Anything you don't like? There are a few specialties here that are really nice."

"Whatever you want to order," I said. "I trust you." The words caught me by surprise as I said them. Why did I trust him? I hardly knew him, and apparently, he had worked for a man like Tomas Barajas. There was a definite tug-of-war happening between my head and my heart.

Our server approached. She also seemed to recognize Gio, but just as he had been with the hostess, he was very professional. They exchanged some pleasantries in Spanish and then he ordered a bottle of wine for us to share, as well as a few appetizers. She smiled at me as she walked away.

"So, you're a regular here, huh?" I asked.

"What do you mean?" he asked.

"Everyone here seems to know you," I said. "Do you bring a lot of girls here?"

He laughed. "No, no. I used to come here all the time for business."

"Ah," I said, teasing him. "Okay, *sure*. I believe you."

"So, you still think I'm a player," he said.

"Well... I mean, look at you," I said. "You're extremely good looking. I'm sure there's no shortage of women throwing themselves at you. You said yourself you're like The Bachelor."

"And you don't have men throwing themselves at you?" he asked. "Anyone at home missing you?"

"No, no one worth mentioning but I'm assuming you already knew that."

"Maybe, but it's part of the job," he said. "I'm sorry if I invaded your privacy."

"I think your job is to invade my privacy." I laughed.

"Is that hard for you?"

"Yes and no," I said. "It's weird because I kind of miss being on my own, but then..." I trailed off, unsure if I should say more.

"What?"

I hesitated and took a deep breath. "But then I like being with you."

"I like being with you too." He smiled at me and took my hand. "Just in case you were worried that you're one of many, let me assure you that you're not."

My words got stuck in my mouth for a moment. "I..."

"And it's not just because you're beautiful," he continued. "It's so much more than that. It's the way you carry yourself. The way you handle yourself in these meetings. You're composed, you're smart, I can tell you're good at your job. You're going toe to toe with some really powerful men and yet you don't seem intimidated."

"I'm still not quite sure how I ended up on such a high-profile job," I laughed.

"I think Jake is rooting for you," he said.

"Speaking of heavy hitters, are you going to tell me about Tomas?" I was not going to miss my opportunity to ask the question.

"You really want to know about him, huh?" He took a deep breath as if he was going to shrug it off.

"I was talking to Ricardo today," I continued. "And he was telling me all about the cart—um... the history of Mexico. And how it's complicated." I tried to give him a meaningful glance, so he'd understand my meaning.

"So, what is it you want to know?"

"I want to know about your *old life* and how you came to be where you are today," I said.

He took a deep breath. "I used to work for Tomas, but it was never a career I wanted," he began. "My family had very little when I was growing up and his family—as I'm sure you have learned—is very powerful in Mexico. They gave me an opportunity to provide for my family when we desperately needed help."

"Are the rumors about him true?" I whispered. Gio nodded. "Is he dangerous?"

"Si."

"Is Sam dangerous?"

"Maybe," he hedged, "But not as long as I'm around."

"Are you dangerous?"

His face scrunched up a bit and I could tell he was hurt by my question. He took a deep breath and then looked into my eyes. "I am not dangerous to you, or your team, no. But if anyone tries to hurt you, or any of your colleagues, I'll kill them."

I sat rooted to the spot, staring into his eyes. It was a moment before I found my voice. "I'm not sure what to say..."

"Are you afraid of me?" he asked.

"No," I answered without hesitation. "So much of this is so new, and I'm realizing how much of a bubble I've been living in my entire life."

"Mexico is beautiful and complicated," he said.

"So are you."

"Come here," he whispered, placing his fingers on the bottom of my chin pulling my lips towards his in what felt like slow motion.

We kissed and then I pulled away and looked at him. "Thank you," I said.

"For what? The kiss? I'm happy to oblige."

"Well, yes," I laughed. "But also, for telling me the truth."

"I don't know any other way," he said.

I kissed him again, deeply this time and when I pulled away and he smiled at me, I knew there was no way I was going to keep questioning things between us. I was putty in his hands.

The rest of the evening was a magical blur of delicious food, amazing wine, conversation, flirtation, kisses, and so much scintillating eye contact. Gio wanted to know my whole story and was particularly interested in why I started speaking Spanish. We slipped back and forth between Spanish and English as we spoke. I had never had so much fun on a date before.

"My mother really wanted me to learn English," he said. "She thought it would give me more opportunities in life. So, I spent a lot of time watching old American movies when I was growing up. Like *Roman Holiday, Casablanca* and *Butch Cassidy and the Sundance Kid...* those helped to teach me English."

"God, you're so cute," I blurted out.

He laughed. "Here's lookin' at you kid." He kissed me again. "So, tell me how you came to speak such good Spanish?"

"So many Americans just take a couple of years for school credit," I said. "But I love being able to speak to different people from different backgrounds and experiencing different cultures. I feel like my ability to speak Spanish has opened many different doors for me. I've studied abroad in Spain twice, because once was not enough, and it's now allowed me the opportunity to work here."

"You have a curiosity to you, don't you?" he said.

"I like to try new things."

We talked about our childhoods, which despite our different upbringings were more similar than I had expected. Teenage crushes, pressure to do well in school and make our parents proud. As we finished our last glass of wine, our server brought the check and Gio reached for it before I had a chance to offer.

I thanked him and kissed him lightly. "Just in case you were worried that you're one of many..." I beamed up at him, "Let me assure you that you're not."

He pulled my face back in and we kissed more passionately.

"Ah, amor!" A voice pulled us out of our moment, and we looked up to find Sam standing over us.

"Sam?" Gio said in a questioning tone. "I'm sure this is just a coincidence?"

"Gio," Sam replied. "Absolutely."

"Well good, we were just leaving. Enjoy your evening."

Gio took my hand and led me out of the restaurant and onto the street.

"What's his deal?" I asked. "Why is he here?"

"He lives in the area," he said. "I've seen him here before."

"Huh..." I wasn't sure how to respond, but Gio's rationale seemed reasonable. He looked into my eyes, and I melted at his gaze.

"Don't worry Bella. He's harmless." As he reassured me, he placed his hand on my lower back and ushered me out of the restaurant. I realized in that moment I would believe anything that he said.

We walked out of the restaurant and made our way down the cobble-stone alley, back to the hotel and my foot wobbled a bit as the heel of my boot caught the stone at an angle.

"These streets don't seem to like my shoes!" I laughed.

Gio laughed too. "Do you need someone to carry you?"

"I think I do!" I joked. But Gio was too quick. He scooped me off my feet and threw me over his shoulder like I didn't weigh anything. "Oh my gosh! Are you serious!?" I squealed.

He carried me a block before he put me down on my feet. "Sorry," he laughed. "I just wanted to show off my strength."

"Well, mission accomplished!"

He took my hand and we walked back to the W together.

We walked into the lobby of the hotel and my heart sank a little at the prospect that our evening together might be coming to an end. He tightened his grip on my hand as if he could sense what I was feeling.

As we passed the bar, I saw Max out of the corner of my eye talking to a lady there. I tried to turn my head, but he spotted me. "Hey Blake!" he called out. "How was your workout?"

"It was good!" I called back, embarrassed. "Night, Max!"

"I see how it is!" He was laughing.

Gio looked at me and at Max and chuckled to himself. "Buenas noches!" he called to Max.

We rode the elevator up together, our fingers firmly intertwined. I leaned my head against his arm and stifled a giggle. "Thank you for tonight," I said. "I had a wonderful time."

"I did as well," he said as the elevator opened. He walked me to my door, and we looked at each other. He leaned down and we kissed again. His hands gripped my waist, and I felt his fingers caress the bear skin on my back just above the waist of my jeans.

"Do you want to come in?" I asked sheepishly.

"I do," he said. "But I know tomorrow is a big day and I don't want to keep you up all night."

I melted a bit at his words. "That's probably a good idea," I said.

"I know some of the team is going back to the U.S. this weekend but why don't you stay? Saturday I can take you to Teotihuacán for the day. I think you'll enjoy exploring another part of the area. Would that be okay?"

"I'd love that," I said. It had been so busy with work I'd completely forgotten I even had the option to go home for the weekend.

"Good," he said.

"Thank you again." I pulled the key card out of my purse and pressed it into the card reader. The light turned green. I turned back to face him. I didn't want him to leave.

He leaned down and kissed me again and then nuzzled his nose against mine. "Don't worry. I'll see you in a few hours," he teased.

"That's true," I giggled. "See you in a few hours."

"Goodnight, Bella."

"Goodnight, Gio."

CHAPTER ELEVEN
Las Mujeres

Standing in front of my wardrobe in my hotel room I fingered through the numerous business suits in varying shades of black and navy blue and was reminded of an internship in college where my manager told me I looked too cutesy in my bright pink dress and may not be taken seriously in the future.

I wondered why it was so hard for women to be taken seriously in a business setting, and why the color of my outfit somehow reflected my knowledge, expertise, and value to the team.

I was lucky that the men that I was working with in Mexico were supportive of me, but there were times at Global Core where I felt like I had to work twice as hard and then be twice as thoughtful in my responses to be respected. Was that just part of paying dues? Or was it some kind of workplace sexism that needed to change? I thought about Lola and how Tomas had spoken to her. How he'd called her la niña, *little girl*, in a meeting in front of all her colleagues, just because she'd pointed out that he needed to stick to the terms he agreed upon when selling off Timbre. Lola had had to just stand there and take it, because she was a woman, and he was a more powerful man.

I chose a charcoal gray pantsuit and white silk blouse for the day. Then I slipped on my glasses instead of contacts. I felt like they made me look more mature.

Today I was running a meeting with the Timbre and Grupo Merced working teams to discuss in more detail the number of people that were still delivering the work for Timbre even though they no longer worked for the same company. We needed to understand how many hours the Grupo Merced team was spending delivering work to Timbre to identify how much PacSouth should pay Grupo Merced for their services. Jake and George were putting their trust in me, and I wanted to make sure everything went smoothly.

I had developed a spreadsheet that had the required information ready to be populated through Excel during the meeting. It was a straightforward, easy process and Chela and Lola would be there with me in case anything went wrong.

As we arrived at the Timbre offices, I set up my computer and prepared to share my screen. I walked through the plan of attack one more time with Chela and Lola and they nodded in agreement.

"You're going to do fantastico," Chela encouraged me.

"Si," Lola chimed in. "You've got this, Blake."

The Timbre and Grupo Merced teams arrived with Sam in tow. I hadn't expected him to be in a meeting with the junior teams, but it wasn't a total surprise that he had shown up. Gio had warned me that part of Sam's job was to intimidate us into giving Grupo Merced what they wanted.

As they sat down Sam made eye contact with me and raised his eyebrows. "You're looking well, Señorita," he said with a sly smile. "Did you enjoy your dinner last night at La No. 20?"

"I did, Sam, gracias," I said feeling bold. "Have you been enjoying all the lurking you're doing these days?"

"¿Que?" Lola looked to me with questioning eyes, but I just waved her off. Then I glanced over at Gio in his usual spot, and he winked at me.

"Buenas dias," I said. "Good morning. Let's get started. ¿Todos hablan Español?" Everyone in the room nodded so I proceeded to run the meeting in Spanish.

We began with a few PowerPoint slides, one stating the objectives of the meeting and the second detailing how we would accomplish our objectives.

"Today's task was to define the number of employee hours that are presently required to deliver a service to Timbre," I said. "So, we'll be wanting to find out from all of you how many hours of work you're currently doing on behalf of Timbre." As I spoke, everyone in the room nodded along and I was feeling confident. I glanced over to Chela and Lola, and they were both smiling at me. Chela gave me a small thumbs up.

"Moving on," I said, clicking over to the Excel spreadsheet to discuss the first service which was Financial Accounting. I asked the group, "How many people in the accounting department are still doing work for Timbre as part of Grupo Merced?"

"I manage that department," said a man in the group. "I can give you a list of names of those who are still doing accounting for Timbre." He started listing names of his colleagues, but Sam cut him off.

"Whoa, whoa, whoa," he said, standing. "You should not be doing *any* work on behalf of Timbre. I thought I made that clear. The Grupo Merced team should no longer be working with or for the Timbre team."

"Now just a moment, Sam—" Lola started to interject.

"If I may," I interrupted her.

She met my eye, and I held up one finger trying to signal to her to give me a moment with him. She nodded.

"Sam, thank you for your valuable feedback, as always," I said to him. I couldn't help the sarcasm that was coloring my words.

He was just so irritating! "Don't worry, we have the same goal here."

"Oh really..." He sneered at me.

"Si, I am simply trying to determine who on your team is doing accounting for Timbre so that Timbre can pay your company back for that service."

"Oh—" He looked dumbfounded. His face was frozen, and his mouth was shaped like a little donut.

"You see, we want to ensure Grupo Merced is not out any money for the work being done on behalf of Timbre."

"Can we move on now?" Lola asked. Everyone in the room nodded.

"Great!" I exclaimed. I looked over to Sam who still looked a little perplexed and I felt satisfied. I shifted my gaze over to Gio who was grinning and stifling a little chuckle. He was proud of me. "Bien, todos. Tenemos otros quince servicios para discutir."

We continued with the meeting, and I went through the remaining fifteen services until we felt we had what we needed. As I spoke, I watched the faces of the group and I realized that they were engaged and smiling. I was providing them with valuable information. I was in command. I was seamlessly running the meeting and I felt proud of myself. By the time we were done I realized that I'd done the entire thing all on my own. I hadn't needed Lola or Chela's help at all. As I thanked everyone for coming and they filed out of the room, I was beaming.

As I was gathering my belongings, Sam walked over to me. I had the impulse to roll my eyes and say, *"What?!"* He was fake and slick. I wanted to get away from his toxic energy as soon as I could.

"Tengo fé en tí, rubia," he said. "Don't make me change my mind."

I felt my blood start to boil at his words. "You *should* have faith in me," I replied hotly. "I'm good at my job."

Before he could respond, Gio appeared at my side. "I'll be showing Sam out, Blake. Gracias."

"Of course, you're here to save the day," Sam said, but Gio only rolled his eyes and showed him the way out.

"You did great," Lola said, approaching me.

"Si! We should go get a drink and celebrate!" Chela added.

As I sat at the table at Contramar with Lola and Chela, my blood was still a little bit hot. "How do you deal with that?" I asked the ladies.

"What do you mean?" Lola asked, taking a sip of her drink.

"The way men are here!" I lamented. "Men like Sam! God! He's so slimy and gross and rude! He's disrespectful. It's infuriating! Ugh!"

"He's just another boy," Chela laughed. "Maybe it's different in the U.S., but here it's still very traditional and it's a machismo culture. Men aren't used to women being in positions of power, so we have to remind them that that's the way things are now." She winked. She seemed relaxed and lose, and far more upbeat than when I had first met her.

"She's right," Lola agreed. "It's just different for women here. There are always going to be some men who are macho, and you must work that much harder to gain their respect. It's important to constantly remind them of the contribution women can make so that they treat you with respect."

"Well, that's crap!" I said offhandedly.

They burst into laughter, and I joined in.

"It is!" Chela said through her giggles. I took another sip of my drink and took a deep breath.

"You're doing great though," Lola said.

"Thanks," I said. "Chela, you seem like you're in a better place than when we first met."

"I am," she said with a smile.

"You seemed sad when I first met you. I didn't want to pry but it's just nice to see you like this."

"I've been going through a divorce," she said. "It was really hard at first, but it's getting better now and I'm feeling good about my choice."

"I'm glad," I said, raising my glass. We toasted again and I took a sip of my drink. "It's so beautiful here." I looked around the room. Trying to absorb the moment, the smells and the people chatting animatedly with each other. Working abroad had always been a dream and I was living it. And I was learning from two amazing women, to top it off. I wanted to soak it all in and freeze the moment in time.

"How do you feel about how the meeting went today?" Chela snapped me back to reality.

"Good," I said. "I felt like it went really well, except for Sam."

Lola laughed. "Don't worry about him."

"You handled yourself well with him," Chela said. "Remember you can't bend to fit his needs. And when he is wrong, you must call him out. Every. Single. Time. And not just Sam, but anyone! You can't be afraid to stand up for yourself."

"And most importantly you must always support your fellow women," Lola added. "That is something I have learned recently." She winked at me.

"Claro que sí. ¡Salud!" Chela said, raising her glass.

"Tomas better watch out because I do not take well to being pushed around by a man," Lola said with a laugh. "I recently went through a divorce too and I do not have the patience for macho men!"

"I didn't know you'd just been through that too," I said. "I'm so sorry!"

"Si," she said "You have to wait for the right person who will support you and your endless pursuit of perfection. Anyone who's not willing to support you isn't worth your time. My husband wanted me to quit my job and just have children and that wasn't the path I wanted. We tried to compromise, but in the end, we went different directions."

"I understand that," I said. "I couldn't be with someone who didn't support me and my career."

Chela looked at me. "My ex didn't want me to work full time, but I needed to live my life for myself and our daughter. He didn't take care of us and if I had left it up to him, we wouldn't have had enough money to survive."

"So, you stepped up," I marveled.

"Si, and now we are free of him, and she and I are okay. We don't need support from anyone else. Everything I do, I do for her—my mini me."

"You're both pretty amazing," I said. "I'm so glad I met you! It can be a little exhausting being with the boys all the time."

"We understand!" Chela said laughing.

"To las mujeres!" Lola said, raising her glass again.

"Blake, ¿Vas a Estados Unidos este fin de semana?" Chela asked.

"No," I said. "I'm actually staying here this weekend."

"A ha..." Chela started to smile. "¿Por que?"

"I just thought I'd spend a little bit of time seeing some more of the city," I said, trying to play it cool. I could tell I wasn't fooling them though.

"¿Sola?" Lola asked. "Are you going to see the city by yourself?"

"Alright!" I finally broke. "I see what you two are up to!"

They laughed.

"It's so obvious!" Chela said giggling. "We see the way he looks at you!"

"But we think it's cute!" Lola said.

I could feel my face turning red. "You guys! You know he might be outside somewhere! He dropped us off here!"

Chela lowered her voice. "So, he's going to take you exploring, huh?"

"Yeah," I smiled. "I'm excited."

"I bet you are excited to explore more than just the city, chica!" Lola exclaimed.

"Lola!" I shrieked and my face exploded in fire.

Chela laughed too and raised a glass. "To Blake's Latin lover! Let's hope he doesn't get too distracted by you to look after the rest of us!"

"I'll make sure he doesn't!" I said, still giggling.

My heart filled with joy as I heard the sound of our laughter reverberating around the restaurant. The sounds of me and my coworkers turned friends, talking about guys, having a girls' night out.

CHAPTER TWELVE
The St. Regis

Gio didn't give too many specifics. All he said was that with things heating up with our negotiations with Tomas that it would probably be a good idea for all of us to move to a more secure hotel. He joined us in the conference room to discuss.

"After the last meeting with Sam, I think we should take additional precautions," he said. "I know the security team at the St. Regis, and I think it might be wise to move you all there."

I wasn't going to argue with him. It was clear that at the very least Sam had been lurking around. He showed up at dinner with Gio and me at La. No 20, and he was clearly pissed after the last meeting. We had no way of knowing if any of Tomas' other guys were lurking around too, clocking our whereabouts and day to day activities.

Charles agreed with Gio and asked if I'd help. "Blake, would you mind calling the St. Regis and asking if we can get a group rate like we had with the W?"

"You don't want Gio to call?" I asked.

"I'm not sure I know everything the team requires," Gio said.

"Right," Charles said. "Blake, you know the kind of accommodations we need. I know you'll make sure we are taken care of."

"When do we need to move hotels?" I asked.

"As soon as possible," Gio said.

"And George, Charles, Max, and I are all flying home for the weekend so if we could move hotels before we leave tomorrow morning that would be ideal."

"No pressure huh?" I said, feeling slightly panicked.

"You've got this," he said. "You're tough, and you speak Spanish. No problem, right?"

"Sure!" I said trying to sound confident.

I spent some time doing online research, and the more I read, the more excited I was at the prospect of moving to the St. Regis. It was a large round building in the middle of La Reforma with a spa and infinity pool on the 34th floor with sweeping views of the city. And that wasn't all.

"A butler service?" I hadn't realized I said it out loud until Max reacted.

"What now?" he asked, leaning over to look at my screen.

"The St. Regis has a butler service. What do you think they do?"

"I've heard about this. I think they'll iron your clothes and shine your shoes," he said. "I am into that!"

By lunchtime, I was so enamored with the idea of moving to the St. Regis that I started to worry I wouldn't be able to make it happen for the team. I had sent an email but was yet to hear back from their corporate relations team.

When Charles checked in with me later that day, I still hadn't achieved my goal.

"Blake, how are we doing with the move?" he asked.

"I'm hoping to hear back soon," I said.

"Okay!" he left the room.

My stomach twisted into a nervous knot, and I decided I needed to get outside. "I'm going to step out for a few and get some air," I told Max. Then I walked out of the room and into the hall. Gio was sitting there reading. He looked up and met my eyes with a smile.

"Everything okay?" he asked. "Did you talk to them?"

"Can we take a walk?"

He nodded and we headed outside. "I have emailed the St. Regis and haven't heard back yet. I'm nervous they won't get back to me."

"Try calling them," he advised. "If you can't get anyone on the phone, I'll take you there after work."

"I can just call and ask for a group discount?" I asked. For some reason I thought that was the sort of thing that should be handled in writing.

"¡Claro, que si!" he said with a laugh. "Sometimes you Americans are too formal."

"Yeah, yeah, yeah...." I nodded and reached for my phone. I pulled up the number, dialed and took a deep breath as it rang.

"¡Buenas dias!" A woman's voice answered the phone. "St. Regis Hotel."

"Hola," I spoke in Spanish. "May I speak with Corporate Relations?"

"Certainly," she said. "Let me transfer you."

I looked up to Gio and his eyes were on me. He raised his eyebrows inquisitively.

"They're transferring me." I whispered. We continued to walk down the street. It was early afternoon, and the sun was beginning to dip lower in the sky. The city was vibrant and bright. I tried to just take it all in and remember where I was. If the St. Regis didn't happen there would be other hotel options for us here.

After another moment the call was picked up again. "Hola, St. Regis corporate relations."

"Hola," I said. "My name is Blake Voss. I'm calling from Global Core Consulting. We are in Mexico City for a multi-month engagement, and we have five prospective full-time residents that we'd like to house at your hotel for the next six months. I wanted to see what kind of rate you might be able to give us? The six-hundred a night is a bit high for our budget."

"Yes, ma'am. I understand," he said. "Let me just check with my superior. One moment please."

"Thank you," I said.

I looked at Gio. He was watching me attentively, his eyes radiating warmth and encouragement. I must have looked nervous because he gave me a small reassuring nod and said, "You got this." I laughed as it wasn't the kind of phrase that was a part of his vernacular, but he knew it was exactly what I needed to hear.

"Miss Voss?" the voice returned to the call.

"Yes."

"We can offer a rate of three hundred dollars a night. Would that work for Global Core?"

"We were really hoping for two hundred and twenty-five dollars a night." I said. This was a rate even lower than what we had at the W.

"Okay, Miss Voss, we can make that work. Under one condition. I would like you to introduce us to your procurement team to encourage other Global Core employees to stay with us when they come to Mexico City."

My eyes got wide and for a moment I could hardly speak. I'd done it! When I finally found my voice again, it practically cracked with delight. I took a deep breath and then smiled wide as I looked at Gio and answered. "That's perfect – I can definitely do that. Thank you! When can we check in?"

"Whenever you like."

Checking into the St. Regis was a moment of personal victory for me. As the team exited our black SUV's in the evening twilight, and began unloading our luggage there were murmurs of excitement and appreciation.

"Wow, Blake! You did good!" Jake praised me.

"This is rad, Blake!" Max chimed in. "Great job!"

"I knew you had this handled," Charles praised me as well. "We are going to be much safer and more secure here."

"And we'll be in the lap of luxury for less than we were paying before!" George said.

"Happy to help!" I felt proud.

We were met at the car port by the butler service and taken up in an elevator to a beautiful lobby with a thirty-foot ceiling and wrap-around balcony where you could see up and down Reforma to El Monumento a La Independencia - el Ángel on the left, and to the right you could see the top of the castle from Chapultepec Park. I felt like I was a princess, walking into the lobby with all the fresh flowers and beautiful aromas.

When we arrived at the front desk, they offered us each a warm towel and glass of champagne. Fresh-squeezed juice was also an option. We opted for the champagne as we felt that we were celebrating. Gio approached the desk and chatted with the concierge staff. They all looked as if they knew him. I sipped my champagne, buzzing with excitement.

"Miss Voss," one of the concierge staff addressed me. "We have you down for five executive suites. Does that work for you?"

My eyes got wide. I took a moment to compose myself. "Yes, that will work nicely, gracias."

I looked at Gio questioningly. "Did you do this?" I mouthed to him. "Suites?"

He raised his eyebrows nonchalantly as if to say, *I have no idea what you're talking about.*

I just smiled and shook my head at him. He was really making it difficult to resist him.

"Alright! Warriors game in an hour?" Max asked the group. "We're still all going to watch right?"

"Sounds good!" Charles said. "Let's all meet back here in an hour."

"Play-off game one, baby!" Max said.

"Wouldn't miss it!" I chimed in.

With room keys in hand, they shuffled us to our respective suites. When I arrived up to my room, there was a plate of warm cookies and a note from the concierge.

Thank you for bringing your team to the St. Regis Mexico City. We are excited to have you here. If you need anything at all, please reach out. You have my number and enjoy your stay.

I was on cloud nine. I couldn't believe the service. The butler, Juan started unpacking my suitcase and hanging my clothes in the wardrobe for me.

"Would you like me to press your outfit for tomorrow?" he asked.

I thought about my pending date with Gio to Teotihuacan in the morning. I had no idea what to wear for that, so I just declined politely. "Not today, maybe next week?"

"Si, no problemo," he said.

I barely ironed my own clothes on a day-to-day basis, but from now on my clothes were going to be wrinkle-free.

Once Juan was done with my suitcase, he gave me a quick tour of the room. There were huge floor to ceiling windows, where I could see everything down La Reforma all the way to Chapultepec Park. There was a large seating area with a sofa in addition to a desk and bed.

"Do you need any extra towels?" he asked me. I looked around the bathroom. It was immaculate with a large overhead rain shower, beautiful sunken bath, and a large vanity. There were marble accents everywhere.

"I think I'm okay for now," I said. "Gracias, Juan."

The room was also technology enabled he showed me how to work the electronic shades, and the light switches from an iPad next to the bed and he showed me a TV which was in the mirror in the bathroom. My mind was fully blown.

"Do you need anything else?" he asked me as we completed the tour.

"I think I'm good but if that changes, I'll let you know."

"Not a problem, Ms. Voss," he said.

"Gracias, Juan."

As soon as he closed the door, I spun around the room, beside myself with glee. I decided to draw myself a quick bath to wash the day off prior to meeting the team for the game.

As I lay in the bath, submerged in the water, it was a total *pinch me* moment. I had made this happen! I had secured a killer rate at the most gorgeous hotel! And it was all because I had asked for what I wanted. I made a note to myself to do that more frequently in the future. The worst someone could say was no, but the upside was far greater.

As I got ready for dinner, I turned on the mirror-TV which was already dialed into a local news station. I went into my closet to pull out an outfit for the evening when I heard the newscaster begin speaking in Spanish about a man who had disappeared.

"José Rivera, who was snatched from his home, joins the ever-swelling ranks of thousands of desaparecidos, victims of the drug conflict that shows no sign of easing."

"Oh no..." I said, staring at the TV, transfixed. It was one of those moments where my excitement about being here conflicted with the realities of the current political crisis. I loved Mexico. The people; the culture; the scenery; the food... but there was an ever-present reminder of the dark side of Mexico that you couldn't ignore when you were here for longer than a week-long vacation, and especially if you were dealing with potential cartel leaders directly. I was thankful we had Gio. I was grateful we were in a safer hotel and that Sam and his people, as of now, didn't know where we were. I turned off the TV and decided to focus on the fun I was going to have with my coworkers tonight. The bad news could wait.

As I walked down to the lobby to meet the team, I couldn't take my eyes off the interior of the hotel. Every bit of it seemed elegant and polished. I felt important just walking in the space. I pictured myself in a ball gown about to dine with the Prime Minister of England, but in reality, I was in a basketball jersey heading to the lobby.

I was thrilled that the team had agreed to watch the Warriors Playoff game together. I had grown up going to countless Warriors games in seasons where they lost more games than they won. It was exciting to have a winning team and while I wished I was in California with my family to watch the game, I was happy that my colleagues had agreed to cheer along with me.

We met in the central lobby and headed into one of the bars in the hotel, where I had been assured by the concierge that the game would be on.

Lola and Ricardo, I had learned, had grown up Bulls' fans having watched Michael Jordan school everyone in the 1990's. And they had taken a real liking to the Warriors.

"I love that you guys are basketball fans!" I said to them.

"I feel like I'm the Steph Curry of our team," Lola joked as we walked into the bar. "I'm leading the charge and making all the big plays."

"I'll agree with that," Ricardo chimed in.

"The team would be lost without you, Chica." Chela said. "Timbre would likely be without basic operating needs like personnel files or even desk chairs without you!"

We entered the bar and found places to sit near a big screen TV.

"I didn't realize you were a player, Blake," Ricardo joked, pointing to my own last name on the back of my jersey.

"The MVP!" I joked back. I looked at Gio and he smiled wide at me.

"Now y'all know that I'm a Lakers fan," Max said. "But we had a very rough season... and I'm really torn up about it." He feigned some tears.

"Awww! You gonna be okay, Maxy?" Jake teased him.

"I'm good, man!" he said. "Blake knows this, but The Warriors are my number two team! So, I'm here for this!"

"Well, thanks for making the sacrifice," I teased him. "We appreciate your second-place fandom."

"I'm a Celtics fan, if you must know," said Charles.

"Boooo!" George was a Knicks fan.

"But my boys are on the other side of the division so tonight, I'll root for Blake's team," Charles laughed.

"Well, I'm a soccer fan," Jake said. "And I gotta eat."

"Right there with you!" Gio joked.

"¡Si!" agreed Chela. "But tonight, GO Blake!"

The server came around with menus and we ordered drinks as the pre-show began.

"Blake, you did an amazing job getting us here," Charles said. "You should see the spa! There is a steam room, sauna, and jacuzzi! I may never go home."

"Well, don't forget you have a morning flight," Jake teased him.

"I almost canceled mine after I saw the size of the bed," George joked. "We definitely should have switched hotels sooner!"

"Why aren't you going home this weekend, Blake?" Charles asked. "First time away from home on a long business deal, I would have thought you'd be itching to go home and see your friends."

"She's hanging with us," Lola said, covering for me.

"Si, we're doing a girls weekend," Chela added.

"How fun!" Charles said.

I looked over to Gio and gave him a tiny wink.

There was a bit of a conflicting feeling about not going home for the weekend. I missed my friends back home and there was part of me that would have loved nothing more than to be hopping on a flight back to Dallas with the sunrise... but then I looked across the table at Gio, and his dark eyes seemed to penetrate my soul. I remembered the way it felt when he had kissed me. His soft, splendid lips...the way his teeth had lightly nibbled on my bottom lip. The way his mouth tasted... the way his hands felt as they gripped me around my waist; the warmth of his body pressed against mine. The idea of spending an entire day with him tomorrow was utterly intoxicating.

My friends back home could wait.

As the evening passed and the game commenced, we all cheered on the Warriors and booed the Cavaliers. We shared food and we shared drinks. It reminded me of being back in Dallas and being out with my best friends for the night.

The Warriors ultimately lost the game that night, but it didn't matter to me, because I was with my team, and they were starting to feel like family.

CHAPTER THIRTEEN
Teotihuacán

After the game, I said goodbye to Max, Charles, Jake, and George and wished them a fun long Easter weekend. I couldn't believe it was already Holy Week. The last few weeks had been a total blur. I went back to my room and within a few minutes my phone rang. It was Gio.

"Well, hi," I answered. "Qué sorpresa!"

"Hola," he said warmly. "I wanted to talk to you about tomorrow."

For a moment my heart stopped, worried that he was about to cancel on me. "Okay..."

"I want to make sure that you wear comfortable shoes since we're going to be hiking, and also bring a water bottle with you. It's going to be hot."

"I can do that," I said. My lips pulled up into a humongous smile as my brain was flooded with images of Gio in athletic wear, his skin flushed slightly from physical exertion. Suddenly, I was very aware of my body.

"I will pick you up at 9AM tomorrow morning, Bella," he said. "I'm excited to show you around."

"I'm excited too," I said. *Very excited.*

"Have sweet dreams," he said. And then we ended the call.

I tossed and turned all night, too excited to sleep. My mind raced, trying to imagine the kind of day that Gio had planned. I knew he wanted to take me to see the pyramids, but knowing Gio, and his constant surprises, I was sure there would be more to it than just that. I imagined kissing him again and thinking about it made my stomach flip with nerves and excitement. When I finally was able to sleep, I had fuzzy, nonsensical dreams that featured shadows and echoes of his face and his voice. It was as if I could feel him but not see him entirely. When I awoke in the morning, I felt soft and dreamy.

I stood in front of the mirror before I dressed and looked at my body. I tried to imagine seeing myself the way he might see me. The curves he'd like, the soft quality of my skin, my freckles. I looked into my own eyes, and it felt like I was seeing someone I didn't recognize. Gio made me feel like a woman, in the truest sense of the word. I had been feeling like a child, trying to keep up with all these older, and more experienced colleagues, but when I was with Gio or he was around, I felt this confidence bloom in me, and it filled me with strength.

"Clearly he's into you," I said attempting to give myself a pep talk. "Just go have fun."

I put on some yoga pants, a tank top, grabbed a light zip up sweatshirt, my water bottle, put on my running shoes and walked downstairs. It was just after eight-forty-five, but I was feeling alert and awake, excited for my day with him. My phone buzzed with a text that he was parked out at valet. As I walked, he was standing outside of his truck by the passenger door, waiting for me.

"Buenas dias, Bella," he said, as he opened the door for me. "Breakfast?" He held up a paper bag with breakfast pastries in it.

"Oh, thank you!" I said as I climbed in and secured my seat belt. He shut the door gently and then walked over to the driver's side door and climbed in next to me. He was freshly showered, and he smelled amazing. I tried to stay composed.

"There's a chai latte for you already in the cup holder," he said.

"Thank you," I lifted the cup and breathed in the comforting aroma. "Are we going straight to the pyramids?"

"I have a little surprise on the way." He grinned at me. "I want to take you to this little family farm that makes tequila."

"Morning tequila?" I asked, laughing.

"Just a little bit." He winked at me, and I felt my heart lift. He was so adorable that it was hard not to melt into a puddle.

I took a sip of the warm beverage and then picked a piece off from one of the pastries. "Guess I better eat!"

"Good idea," he said.

As we drove out of the city, I watched the scenery around us change. In one area there would be slick high-rise buildings and as we drove outside the heart of the city there were tattered looking shacks stacked up the hillsides. It filled me with a mixture of sadness and confusion. This juxtaposition of beauty and poverty. It was unsettling. I supposed this happens in any major city, but the contrast here was so abrupt that it took me by surprise.

"It's amazing how many people live in this city," I marveled, looking up the hillside.

"Yes" he replied. "Those are the favelas." *Shanty towns.*

"I thought those only existed in Brazil," I remarked.

"We have them here too. There are twenty-one million people living in the greater Mexico City area," he said. "The city does not have enough space for all of the people and many families live with their grandparents, parents and siblings to help take care of one another as well as to avoid the high costs of living."

"Wow," I was unsure of what else to say.

"It's not so bad," he assured me. "Mexican families are traditionally very close, and it's an honor to take care of your family."

I thought about that, the bittersweetness of it all settling into my chest. On the one hand, I knew the upsides to a close-knit community, I often wished I lived closer to my family. But I couldn't help thinking about the living conditions inside these homes. As if he sensed my mood shift, Gio reached over and squeezed my hand. I looked to him, and we shared a sweet smile.

As we drove out of the city limits, Gio turned on the radio and I felt myself relax into my seat. It felt good to be with him in this setting. I liked that he was taking me somewhere special. Leading me somewhere he knew I'd like to go. "Whose farm are we heading to?" I asked.

"Some friends of mine," he answered. "It's my godfather's family actually."

"Oh!" I felt surprised that he was introducing me to his family. I must have made a face because he quickly chimed back in.

"Don't worry, you'll like them," he said.

"But will they like me?" I asked. "La rubia from the States?"

"Of course," he chuckled. "Who wouldn't like you!?"

"Sam?" I hedged.

"Well, that's because Sam is foolish."

"You have some history with him, don't you?"

"Bella..." he grumbled.

"There's a story there. I know there is!"

He laughed. "You are quite perceptive."

"That's right," I teased him again. "I'm not gonna press you on it today, because this is a fun day, but at some point, you're gonna have to tell me the whole story."

"At some point, I will," he said. "You have my word."

I reached my hand over to shake his and instead he pulled it up to his lips and kissed me.

"Don't think you can make me forget by being all charming and sweet," I warned him playfully.

He just chuckled and shook his head.

When we eventually pulled up to the farm, we were greeted with warm hugs from everyone.

"Todos, this is Blake," Gio said.

"Hi!" I exclaimed. "Mucho Gusto. Nice to meet you."

"Mucho gusto," they said. There were many hands to shake and hugs to receive.

"Gio!" A handful of little kids were so excited to see Gio that they were clambering all over each other just to be first in line to be tossed in the air by him. It was hard not to smile watching the way he was with the children. *If only men understood that watching them play with children tugs at a woman's heart strings.* I thought.

I thanked them all in Spanish for letting us visit and Gio's godfather, Jaime seemed impressed.

"Ella habla Español!" he said to Gio, complimenting my Spanish speaking abilities. "Bien echo,"

"Si, claro," Gio said.

I could feel myself blushing, "Gracias." I responded.

"Gio, mi casa es tú casa," Jaime said. "¡Qué lo paséis bien!" *Enjoy yourselves.*

"Gracias," I said, thanking him for his hospitality.

"This way, Blake," Gio said, as he took my hand and walked me around the farm.

"Mucho gusto," I called again to Jaime and his family.

The property was expansive and beautiful. There were agave plants growing in neat rows as far as the eye could see. Gio, took me into the field and showed them to me. He pulled a small pocketknife out of his pocket and showed me how to slice the leaf in half so you can see the agave liquid. "There are only five states in Mexico that are legally allowed to produce Tequila... Jalisco, Tamaulipas, Michoacan, Nayarit and parts of Guanajuanto, he said. "If it's made in other areas, it's technically not tequila. So, since we are in the state of Mexico, this is something different."

"So, it's like Champagne in France?"

"Yes, exactly. Jaime and his family, however, leverage the Mezcal making process here and have been producing Mezcal and agave syrup for more than fifty years."

"Does it taste sweet right out of the plant?"

"Not yet," he says. "To make the syrup it has to be reduced."

"How do they do that?" I asked.

"I'll show you," he said, leading me away from the fields.

We walked to the other side of the property where the buildings were. As we passed the workers, they all seemed to know him and waved. Eventually we made it into what looked like the distilling building.

"Over there you can see the traditional pits where the agave plants or piñas are slow roasted in the ground and cooked by wood fire." Gio said as he pointed to his right. "This is one of the key differences in making tequila and Mezcal, as the agave from tequila is typically slow-roasted in ovens and this is why Mezcal typically has a smokier taste."

"I never realized there were so many different kinds," I said sheepishly. "I always just thought there was tequila in margaritas, or in shot glasses."

"You're not the only one," he said. "It's a common misconception. But that's what makes it so fun to learn about."

He led me inside and I sat on a stool near a small table.

"Ready to taste?" he asked me.

"Breakfast of champions!" I joked.

First, we tried a blanco tequila, a reposado mezcal, and finally an añejo mezcal. He took great pleasure in describing the differences of all three of them to me.

"Blanco, or silver as the gringos call it, is barely aged more than a couple of weeks," he explained. "Which makes it the purest of all but not the most interesting tasting. The reposado is aged in oak usually so it's a bit richer in color and flavor, but the añejo has been aged for a matter of years, which mellows out the flavor. This is why most people prefer to sip añejo."

With that he handed me a small glass. I sipped it slowly, wanting to be mindful of the long day we had ahead of us. "Mmm, this is so nice," I said.

"Isn't it?" he sipped his as well and then we smiled at each other like we had a secret.

"Sipping tequila before noon and *then* we're going hiking?" I squealed. "I hope I can walk!"

"If you can't, I'll carry you," he joked. "Are you ready to go? Or do you want to keep drinking?"

"No, no, let's go. I'm excited for what's next."

We walked back through the fields, and I paid special attention to the warmth of the sun on my skin.

"It's such a beautiful day," I said.

"That might be the añejo talking," he teased me.

"Either way I'm happy!" I laughed.

We got back into the car, and I was feeling rosy. There was a pleasant spring breeze blowing as we drove away from the farm. My stomach rumbled slightly but I ignored it and reached for the remnants of my breakfast pastries.

After a short drive, we arrived at the avenue of the dead, and I saw the pyramids.

"Oh my god..." I could hardly speak. I knew what to expect. I'd seen them in photos, but being there in person, I was completely blown away by the grandeur of them. It felt like I was existing in a dream or had been blasted into the past somehow. It was that feeling you get when you see something historic and vast, like the Eiffel Tower or the Roman Coliseum and realize you are so small compared to its sheer timelessness.

"This is Teotihuacan! A very special place," Gio said as we got out of the car. His voice sounded like a child opening his Christmas presents. He was nerding out and it was adorable. "These pyramids are said to have been constructed by the Aztecs around 200 BC."

"I don't even know what to say," I stammered. "They're amazing."

"Aren't they?" He gazed up at these giant stone structures with reverence. "There are three pyramids. The Pyramid of the Moon, The Temple of the Feathered Serpent, and our destination—The Pyramid of the Sun."

We walked toward the enormous pyramid and as we started to climb the steps, I noticed how steep they were, and that some of them were even cracked and broken in parts. I made sure to tread carefully. I didn't want to be the American girl who fell off an Aztec pyramid, and then ruined her second official date with such a dreamy guy. Gio, reached back to help me in places where the stones weren't as stable and every time, he touched my hand, I felt my cheeks warm a little bit.

When we finally got to the top, I looked out over the land, and I practically giggled with happiness. Seeing the views; the other pyramids in the distance, I felt my heart swell. My love for this country was growing exponentially by the day. I was starting to feel an even bigger pull towards Mexico City, and I wanted everyone to know how much I loved this place and how much I wanted to be a part of it.

Gio seemed to notice my emotion and he put his arm around me. "It's beautiful, isn't it?"

"It's overwhelming," I said. "I want to belong here."

"You do belong here," he said. "You belong anywhere you want to be." He kissed the top of my head and tightened his grip around my waist. I leaned into his body and rested my head against him, and in that moment, I felt completely at peace.

When we got back down from the pyramid, Gio took me by the hand and led me away from the stairs and farther along the park. He said he had one more thing he wanted to show me. We walked toward what looked like an amphitheater and he told me that it was a place where the Aztecs used to host ceremonies.

"Stand here," he said, letting go of my hand.

"Okay." I gazed up at him, curious what was about to happen.

"Now clap," he instructed me.

I clapped my hands, and the sound bounced off all the stone structures and echoed multiple times. I looked at him in amazement. I clapped twice and both claps resounded off the stone.

"How in the world...?"

"The Aztecs mastered acoustics before anyone else," he said.

"Wow."

Gio took my hand and walked me all over the Avenue of the dead, and showed me the other pyramids, as well as the old clay homes of the Aztec people. He knew so much about the history. I felt proud knowing I had the best tour guide in all of Mexico.

After we saw the Pyramid of the moon, we stopped to have a drink of water and my stomach rumbled loudly again. "Ready for lunch?" he asked, chuckling.

"I am!" I exclaimed.

"Great! I know just the spot!" he said.

I wasn't surprised.

CHAPTER FOURTEEN
El Sombrero

While my rumbling stomach had hoped that Gio was going to take me somewhere close to the pyramids for lunch, his plan was to drive back to CDMX for a late lunch.

He graciously took me back to the hotel so I could take a quick shower and change. I nibbled on a few almonds I had in my room to tide myself over before our meal.

When he arrived back at the hotel to pick me up, Gio looked freshly shaven and when he hugged me, he smelled like aftershave. The knot of longing in my stomach started to tighten again.

We ended up at a little spot downtown called La Casa de Las Sirena's, which overlooked the city center. There was a balcony tucked away, just out of sight of any tourists' view and inside, there was a sweet, older woman making warm tortillas fresh on a stone pedestal near the tables.

When the server arrived, Gio asked me if I would be comfortable if he ordered for us. I nodded and so he ordered us some of the local favorites and drinks.

"Wow," I said, looking around. "This is such a great spot!"

He smiled and shrugged, looking a little smug.

As the sun started to dip lower in the sky and the tequila started to soften my view, I looked over at Gio and grinned. "This has been a really great day," I said. "Thank you."

"It's my pleasure," he said. "But it's not over yet."

We sipped our drinks and watched the tourists in the city square. He reached over and intertwined his fingers with mine, and then he pulled my hand up toward his lips and kissed it.

When our food finally arrived, I hungrily sunk my teeth into my first bite. I nearly moaned as the flavors hit my tongue and he chuckled.

"What?" I said, through my chews. "You make a girl climb a pyramid and drink mezcal before noon, she's gonna be ready to eat!"

"Of course!" he exclaimed as he dug in.

Plate after plate of food arrived, each dish tastier than the last. We sipped another round of drinks and watched the views until the sun began to set. At six o'clock, the Mexican Color Guard came into El Zócalo, and we had a front row seat to watch the flag lowering ceremony. There must have been at least forty soldiers that were there to participate. Watching them file into the square I felt excited, like a kid watching a July Fourth parade. Together they lowered the enormous Mexican flag, and then began folding it, while someone played a snare drum in the background.

Watching them work, I felt my heart swell in the same way it had standing atop the Pyramid of the sun. The city was full of so much history and tradition. It took my breath away.

I looked at Gio and he just sat there beaming at me.

"This is so amazing!" I exclaimed, watching. "They do this every day?!"

"Twice a day!" he said.

I shook my head in astonishment and watched as they rolled up the flag and then carried it out of the square.

"I love this city!"

When we finished our meal, Gio led me out of the restaurant and onto the street. I felt my heart drop at the thought that the day was coming to a close and my pulse quickened at the thought that we might be spending the night together. *Would he come up to my room? Or would he just walk me to my door like a perfect gentleman?*

"So..." I said. "What now?"

"I have one more surprise for you," he said.

"You just keep 'em coming!"

We walked through the streets toward yet another mystery destination. My mind was racing again, wondering where he was taking me, but the city was so alive that I hardly had time to give it much thought. Everyone was out enjoying their Saturday night. People were chatting animatedly in sidewalk cafes. Others were walking in the streets with friends or loved ones. There were young people, older people, families, couples, tourists were snapping photos. Locals on bicycles whizzed past us. It was electric.

Finally, we reached Plaza Garibaldi where there were dozens of mariachi bands playing. People were dancing in the street and the energy was infectious. Gio looked down at me to gage my reaction and I couldn't help but laugh.

"Should we dance?" he asked.

"Yes!" I exclaimed. Never in my life had a man actually asked me to dance. Even at school dances growing up, the boys would often just slide up and start dancing near the girls, but never like this. Never a true, *shall we dance?* moment. I was elated.

Gio reached for my hand, and I gave it to him. He twirled me and then pulled me in closer to his chest. We swayed to the beat, and he tightened his hand around my waist. I felt like I was living a fairytale.

After a few minutes he twirled me back out so that we were side by side and then we walked along the street hand in hand. We wandered around the area, listening to the different bands.

Occasionally, Gio would twirl me again. I couldn't stop giggling. There were street vendors everywhere selling flowers, toys, food, the streets were busting at the seams.

"¡Señor! ¡Señorita! ¿Te gusta comprar un sombrero?" a particularly enthusiastic street vendor asked if we'd like to buy a hat. He lifted the hat, a cowboy-style Stetson. It was brown felt with a pretty design embroidered around the rim. He held it up to show us all of its fine qualities.

"He really wants to sell us a hat," I said to Gio, giggling.

"A hardworking businessman!" Gio laughed.

I walked toward the stand and looked at a brown hat and then at Gio. "I think this one has your name on it." I reached into my purse and pulled out some money.

The vendor reached for it excitedly. "Perfecto! Great choice!"

I took the hat and put it on Gio's head. He looked awkwardly charming, and I couldn't help but lean up and kiss him. He leaned into the kiss, deepening it all while removing the hat from his head and placing it firmly on mine.

"I think it looks better on you!" he chuckled. "Let's go!"

The rest of the evening passed in the most blissful blur. We spent hours walking around and dancing until our feet hurt. There was another round of drinks at another local bar, there was street corn, there was flan, there were more kisses and so many laughs. I'd never enjoyed myself so much with another person anywhere in the world.

Just as I started to feel tired and ready to head back, Gio took my hand and leaned into my ear. "Should we go?" he asked.

I was so ready. "Yes."

We headed back to the hotel. Me still wearing Gio's new hat, my cheeks rosy from the drinks and dancing.

We walked into the lobby hand in hand heading toward the elevator bank.

This time I didn't leave it to chance. Before we even got to the elevator, I turned to him and looked him square in the face. His eyes were soft. He looked sweet and vulnerable. A little drunk, a little sleepy, smiling down at me.

"Thank you for a wonderful day," I said.

"My pleasure," he said. For a moment I saw his expression fall slightly, like perhaps he thought I was dismissing him.

Then I leaned up and kissed him slowly, biting his lip slightly. I heard him inhale sharply and felt his hands grip my waist.

"Come with me," I said to him. His lips curled into a mischievous smile as I took him by the hand and led him to the elevator. We rode the elevator in silence again. This time he interlaced his fingers with mine. My eyes were soft and dreamy from the evening, and each time I blinked them it felt long and languid. My heart was beating fast...every inch of my skin felt like a live wire. There was no question of how this night was going to end. It was something I'd wanted badly, something I'd fantasized about so many times and now it was finally happening.

The doors to the elevator opened and we walked toward my room. Every step felt like it was in slow motion. I unlocked the door and he followed me inside. The second I heard the lock click behind me, I turned around and in that instant his lips were on mine. I moaned slightly as he lifted me off the ground and I wrapped my legs around his waist. He carried me over the bed and then tossed me onto the soft mattress as if I weighed nothing. I giggled as I landed with a soft bounce, I looked up at him. He removed his shirt and I gazed at his bronzed skin and muscular physique.

"Do you want me?" he asked, crawling onto the bed next to me.

"Yes," I answered without hesitation. I'd never wanted anything more.

CHAPTER FIFTEEN
Más Trabajo

Monday was one of those rare mornings where I woke up naturally before my alarm, feeling cozy and fully rested. I stretched my arms out and smiled thinking about the morning before, when I'd woken up wrapped up in Gio's arms.

"Good morning, Bella," he'd said as he placed a kiss on my bare shoulder.

We had passed so many hours that morning lazily staying in bed, talking, laughing, exploring each other. It was so new; it thrilled me.

The memories were swirling around in my mind as I climbed out of bed to get into the shower. It was so nice knowing that I didn't need to rush into the office. My colleagues were flying back from The States, and they wouldn't be getting into the office until later. I was embracing the Mexican way.

As I stood there under the hot water, memories from the previous morning's shower flashed back into my mind and I couldn't help but smile to myself. Gio's strong hands on me, Gio's lips on mine, steam, hot water, and soap suds everywhere. The memories were intoxicating.

I felt flushed and a little dreamy as I got ready for the day. I took extra time doing my hair and makeup, wanting to look extra cute when I saw him today.

Just before ten o'clock, I heard a knock on my door. When I peeped through the hole, there he was in his cowboy hat holding coffees. I answered the door. "This is a surprise!" I leaned up and kissed him without hesitation.

"I figured since the others would be coming from the airport that I'd come get you and take you out for breakfast before we go into the office."

"Nice hat," I remarked with a smile.

We kissed again and I felt the impulse to drag him into my room and kill an hour in bed, but my stomach growled, reminding me I needed to eat.

He took my hand. "I know we can't do this in front of the others, but for today, is this okay?"

I squeezed his hand and beamed up at him. "Yes, it's perfect." We walked toward the elevators hand in hand.

"Do you think they know?" Gio asked as we entered the elevator. He reached down and pressed the lobby button. The elevator doors closed.

"Some of them do," I said. "Max, Chela and Lola for sure. The other's I'm not sure."

"I think they have an idea," he said with a laugh.

"So, basically everyone knows," I said echoing his laugh.

"Most likely," he conceded, laughing too. "Is that a problem for you?"

"No. I just hope the team knows it won't affect my work." I responded. "Is it a problem for you?"

"I don't think so," he said. "There is nothing in my contract about dating. I just can't let my affections for you get in the way of monitoring the rest of the team's safety."

"But what about after hours?" I said seductively.

He leaned down and kissed my ear lobe softly and then he whispered, "After hours, I'm all yours."

A slight gasp escaped from my lips. The elevator doors opened, and he walked out. I just stood there, still a little bit stunned by his sex appeal.

"Blake, are you coming?" he asked with a wink.

It was around one o'clock in the afternoon by the time that the rest of the team started to trickle into the office. We exchanged a few pleasantries about their time at home, but the relaxed vibe of the morning ended abruptly when it became apparent that it was going to be a long week.

Jake called a team meeting right away so we could discuss all the time sensitive and pressing issues with the deal. We sat around the table with our notepads handy. It was clear it was go time.

"We need to finalize headcount requirements and costs for the TSAs within the next two weeks and we still have four functions to go," he said. "To do this, we need to host meetings daily with the Timbre team and get time with the Grupo Merced working teams to validate our findings."

I suddenly felt very overwhelmed and the sobering realization that I was here for work and not just to gallivant around the city with Gio hit me again.

"Great," said Max. "Seems doable." I wasn't sure if he was being sarcastic.

"Once this is all done, we need to develop the final presentation and prep for our next meeting with Tomas and Sam," said George. "It's going to be a long one today."

"Right," Jake agreed. "Our biggest challenge is going to be the network TSA's, they are complex. We have to tread carefully here with the Grupo Merced team because the network towers are operated in what we believe is cartel land and the network towers are also the most important asset to the Timbre and PacSouth teams. This is the money maker. Ricardo will take point on this with input from Lola and myself."

I made a mental note to pick Ricardo's brain on the intricacies of the network TSA for my own understanding—terms like LAN and network cables were all like speaking a foreign language to me.

"Let's break into teams," Jake said. "Blake and Chela; Max and George; Lola, Ricardo and myself."

"I'll be in the office next door working out some details with the U.S. team," said Charles. "Let's meet back in a few hours to see where we are. Great work, team!"

With that we all jumped up and got to work. Chela and I went to our own little corner to work, spreading out notes from all our previous meetings and opened up our excel spreadsheets. We divided up our responsibilities so we could accomplish this more quickly. I began translating info from our excel spreadsheets into a PowerPoint presentation for the meeting.

As I worked, I started to notice a couple inconsistencies. I scanned over the information, and it became clear that we had a problem with the office space TSA.

"I just realized we do not have a TSA in place for the facilities that the Timbre team is utilizing," I said to Chela.

"We don't?"

"No."

"What should we do?" she asked.

"We should ask how the Timbre and PacSouth team will want to manage this."

"We should talk to Charles," she said. "Knowing Grupo Merced, they will likely overcharge the Timbre team for the use of space, but I also know it is a challenge to find new office spaces and get them set up."

"Okay, I'll get him." I walked into the other office where Charles was sitting.

"Hey Blake," he said when he saw me. "What's up?"

"Do you have a minute?" I asked.

"I've got five," he said.

"Great, can you come talk to Chela and me?"

"Sure." He followed me into the other room.

Chela pulled up the paperwork we had been looking over. "Charles, are you aware of any additional office space for the Timbre/PacSouth team from their current and or new operations?"

"Hmm." He looked thoughtful. "The PacSouth team has old offices in Mexico City, but the offices aren't big enough to support the team in the short term. Why?"

Chela and I exchanged a look. "We don't have a TSA in place for the office space that Timbre is currently using."

"We don't?" he asked.

"No," I said. We showed him the paperwork. "Is this going to present a problem for us?" I asked.

"Well, maybe not," he said, scanning the document. "I believe they are working to secure larger office space and should have offices secured within the next few months."

"Months?" Chela, balked. "What will they do in the short term?"

"Well, let's see if we can get some coverage for the them and let's try and work with Carlos to understand how much time is needed or if they have an alternate plan in mind," Charles suggested. "Blake, can you be sure to add that to the agenda for the meeting tomorrow?"

"Of course," I said.

I updated the slide with Charles' proposal and added any open questions or areas for further discussion. Once completed, I reviewed the slides with Chela.

I felt time bend as we got sucked deeper into the black hole of work. It became hypnotic and I didn't even think about what time it was until I felt myself yawn. I looked at my watch and my eyes grew wide when I saw that it was nearly ten o'clock. We'd been working for hours without a break and without any food.

"Should we get a snack?" I asked Chela.

"Si," she said. "Tengo mucho hambre. My stomach is growling."

We walked to the vending machine down the hall to get ourselves something to eat. I stretched as we looked at what our options were and then Chela and I made our selections.

Our hands were full of chips and candy and caffeinated drinks by the time we started to walk back to our table. Anything to help us stay alert and awake while we finished. We passed Gio in the hallway, in his chair reading a book. He smiled up at me sympathetically and gave me a nod of encouragement. I returned the smile.

"How was your weekend?" Chela asked me, with a little smirk on her face as we returned to our desks.

I had to fight the temptation to gush to her. "It was pretty wonderful," I said, trying not to squeal.

"You will have to tell me more later when we're done with this," she said.

"Another girls night?" I suggested.

"¡Si!"

It was nearly midnight before Charles told us we should go home for the night. "We all know that tomorrow is going to be a big one," he said. "Let's get some sleep so we are all on our A game tomorrow."

Most of us walked out of the office with further stacks of paperwork to review back in our hotel rooms. The blissful feeling, I had woken up with, felt a world away.

As Gio walked us into the St. Regis, he gently rested his hand on my back. It felt nice to be touched affectionately after such a long day. I wanted him to come upstairs with me, but I knew I needed sleep.

"Get some rest, Bella," he said softly as I got into the elevator.

Once in my room, changed clothes and got into bed. I opened my phone for the first time all day to see a text from Mia back at home thanking me for the bottle of champagne I'd sent her for her birthday. I had completely forgotten that today was her day. Time had become such a blur, and my relationships with my friends and family back home, felt like they belonged in someone else's life. I texted Mia back and then felt my eyelids start to sink down as sleep pulled me under.

CHAPTER SIXTEEN
La Pelea

My alarm went off and I jolted awake, feeling like I'd slept no more than five minutes. I was glad I had gotten so much rest over the weekend because the next few days promised to be stressful.

I forced myself to get up and into the shower and desperately turned the tap to the cold side to try to wake myself up further. I never did well on less than eight hours of sleep.

Once dressed, I called the butler service to deliver a double shot of espresso to my room. I drank it as I dried my hair and silently prayed that I'd become more alert with every stroke of the brush.

There was still a huge stack of paperwork on my desk that I hadn't gotten to last night. I brought it into the bathroom and did my best to glance over it as I did my makeup. Finally, after only nearly stabbing my eye with my mascara wand twice, I was ready to head out the door. My hands were shaky from the caffeine, but at least I was alert.

Our office was buzzing that morning as we waited for the Timbre and Grupo Merced teams to arrive. Max was working to make sure our presentations would be flawless. It was the first time the Mexico City team had arrived at the same time as we did. Everyone knew this was an important day. Charles and Ricardo went over notes from the meetings with the Timbre employees. George, Chela, and I double and tripled checked the numbers and assumptions we had been working on with the Timbre teams. In the corner of the room, I could hear Jake and Lola speaking in hushed voices.

"Please don't go off script this time," Jake pleaded with her. "This approach needs to be very calculated, and we need to be careful."

"Jake," she said. "We need to do what is best for our client, and sometimes that means holding a hard line with these people."

"We can hold a hardline," Jake said. "But we need to be subtle about it. I don't want anything bad to happen."

"Yes, subtle," she said. "I agree with you."

After a while we were alerted that Efrain and his team had arrived and they were shortly followed by Tomas, Sam and their people. As they sat down, Sam made eye contact with me and raised his eyebrows.

"Good to see you again, Señorita," he said with a sly smile.

I rolled my eyes.

Once everyone was seated, Jake nodded at Max and our presentation was illuminated on the screen on the wall of the conference room. I felt everyone in the room collectively inhale as we began the meeting.

"So," Jake began. "We want to begin today by discussing the path forward for Timbre as it moves completely over to PacSouth—"

"We'd like to begin by discussing our terms for the TSA's," Tomas interrupted. "Sam will go ahead and outline some numbers for you."

This was a surprise. I looked over to Jake confused and he looked as dumbfounded as I felt.

"Gracias, Tomas," Sam said. He flipped open a folder and started filing through some paperwork. I looked at the rest of the team. George, Max, Charles, Chela, and Ricardo all looked confused, but Lola looked irate. I could see her blood pressure beginning to rise and watched her mumble something under her breath. It was our job to lead the presentation today... everyone knew that, and Tomas was making a power play to try and control the merger. Sam cleared his throat. "Here is what we're prepared to offer."

"Excuse me," Lola jumped in. "This is not the purpose of this meeting. We are here to discuss the terms we are presenting on behalf of our client. This is not an opportunity for you to take control of the meeting, Sam."

There was silence in the room. I glanced over at Jake again, who looked immediately panicked.

"Sam, if you don't mind," he interjected. "We'd like to present our points first and then we welcome an opportunity for your team to counter."

"We do not have time for that," Sam protested.

"If you read the meeting agenda," Lola jumped in again. "You would know the plan was that *we* present to Grupo Merced what Timbre needs in the short term to transition to PacSouth. That's it. That's why we're here."

"I am not here to listen to this woman run her mouth," Tomas said coldly. "That's not why *I'm* here."

"Excuse me," Charles stood as he spoke. "I've been pretty quiet because I'm not a native Spanish speaker, but I will not allow my team to be spoken to that way. Tomas, you are here today at *our* pleasure, to hear what your colleagues need to move into this new chapter, and we expect that to be treated with some respect. If you don't want to hear the terms here in our office as presented by my team, and that includes Lola, then we would be happy to send them to you in writing so you can take the time you need to digest it all before we speak again."

Silence fell over the room again.

"Alright," Tomas said quietly. His teeth clinched. "Please send it to our office in writing so we can read it over. Then we will be in touch."

"We'll prepare the documents right away," Jake said.

As Tomas stood up, he glared at Lola. I watched her hold his gaze until he looked away and walked out the room. She was impressive.

As Tomas and his people began to file out of the room, he doubled back and spoke to Lola. His voice was hushed, but I heard enough to understand what he was saying. *I'd be careful or you might find yourself in a bad situation.*

I watched Lola's face fall a bit at his words. She was doing her best to remain calm, but I could tell that she was a little bit shaken.

Jake stormed over to Lola, "What the hell was that?"

Lola looked at him wide eyed. "Pardon me?" she said.

"You didn't stick to the plan!" he said.

"Neither did he!"

"We said *subtle!*" Jake exclaimed.

"Men like Tomas don't understand subtle," Lola spat out.

"Jake, please," Charles walked over and placed a supportive hand on Lola's shoulder. "This is not the time to discuss this. Both of you are fired up. Let's let everyone settle down and then we can ensure everyone is on the same page."

"Okay good. Team, we need to get ahead of this and get to Carlos," George said.

"I'm on it," said Jake.

"No Jake," Charles interjected. "You get some air. Blake, George and I will call him."

Jake looked furious as he stormed out of the room.

CHAPTER SEVENTEEN
Carlos

Charles, George, and I jumped on the phone with Carlos and told him we needed to meet. It turned out that Efrain wanted to be a part of the debrief as well, so we all went over to his office to have a meeting with him and further strategize. Lola came along with us, while Jake stayed behind, still pouting.

I had hoped that Carlos might be pleased, or even impressed that we'd put it all on the line for them, but when we delivered the news to him, he looked flustered.

"How did this happen?" he asked.

"It was my fault," Lola said, sounding defeated. "I was too direct with Tomas."

"Direct, but correct," I whispered under my breath.

"What was that?" Carlos asked me.

I took a deep breath. "I said that she was correct in what she said to Tomas."

"Honestly I agree with Blake," George jumped in. "Sam tried to derail the meeting and Lola stood up to him. We need them to know that they are not running this show."

Carlos heaved a heavy sigh. "What we *need* is to finish the merger," he said, clearly irritated. "And these kinds of issues don't help things. Now they're angry. I don't want to deal with an angry Tomas Barajas."

"With all due respect," Lola interrupted, "Tomas' reputation is widely known, you had to know that this was a risk when doing business with him."

"That's not the point señorita," Carlos replied.

"I actually think it *is* the point,"George continued standing up for Lola again. "And to be honest, I would have liked to have known his reputation before I arrived here. No one is set up for success unless we know the full truth about what we're walking into."

I decided to pile on. "I feel safer knowing that he is intimidated by Lola. At least he knows our team has boundaries."

Carlos took a deep breath. Then he turned to Gio. "What do you think?" he asked.

Gio cleared his throat. "I think that we're still okay, but it might be best to have fewer meetings with Tomas present."

"What do we do now?" I asked.

"I'll call Tomas," Carlos said as he hit the speaker phone button on his desk phone. "I'll see if I can smooth things over." We all stood in silence as Carlos dialed.

When Tomas' secretary answered, Carlos asked to speak with him and she responded, "¿Estás Seguro?" *Are you sure?*

I looked to Lola. She looked nervous but she stood up straight and tall.

"Si," Tomas came on the line.

"Hola, Tomas, este es Carlos de PacSouth," he said.

They spoke exclusively in Spanish, but I understood Tomas saying that he wouldn't meet with us again if *la niña* was there. We all knew he meant Lola. Even Charles and George's heads swiveled to Lola when he said this.

Carlos told Tomas he understood his frustrations and he would discuss it with us.

"No me gusta ella," Tomas said. "Ella es una perra necesita una correa."

I looked at Lola and she looked like she'd been punched in the gut. Calling a woman a bitch who needed a leash was an enormous slap in the face, even for someone as strong as Lola.

"It's okay," I mouthed to her. "We got you."

Carlos' didn't respond. He couldn't seem to find the words. He avoided addressing Tomas' insult and quickly ended the call in a pleasant tone. As he hung up the phone, he spoke to us again. "For now, let's hold off on taking any more meetings with them until he cools down a bit."

We all nodded in agreement.

"Thanks for your time, Carlos," Charles said. We began filing out of the room.

"Charles, can you hang back for a second? I'd like to speak with you privately," Carlos said.

We walked out of the office somberly.

Charles arrived at the office shortly after we did. He gave us a few remaining tasks to accomplish before he told us to go home and get some rest. It was abundantly clear that he'd taken one for the team with Carlos, but he was too kind to let us know.

Jake stayed behind to work late but the rest of us accepted Charles invitation to go home for the night.

I left the office feeling nervous and beat down. We'd taken a huge loss today and it was the first time since arriving in Mexico City that I started to question whether we actually had what it took to complete this deal, in the right way for our clients.

When the team got back to the St. Regis, Gio was on the phone, so we sort of waved goodnight to each other as I got in the elevator with Max and George.

I entered my room, got changed into comfortable clothes and crashed down on the bed. For a few moments I just laid there allowing the events of the day to wash over me. I was frustrated that Grupo Merced was making the merger so difficult. It was frustrating that we had to endure the egos of Tomas and Sam, and it was even more frustrating that Lola was being treated so disrespectfully simply for doing her job. I thought about the way that even Jake had spoken to her and that upset me. I wanted him to apologize to her, but I knew it wasn't my place to get involved. My stomach rumbled and I realized I hadn't eaten all day. I started flipping through the room service menu when my phone rang. It was Gio.

"Hi," I said tenderly.

"Hola," he said, matching my tone. "How are you?"

"Hungry," I replied. "I'm trying to decide what I want for dinner. I need some comfort food. Today was rough."

"I bet you are very hungry," he said. "I noticed you barely ate all day."

"You are right, I'm starving." There was a knock at the door. "Hold on, Gio, someone's at my door."

"Okay," he said.

I climbed out of bed, wrapped a sweater around me and went to the door. But when I peeped through the hole, all I could see was Gio's shit-eating grin. His hands were behind his back, hiding something. A smile spread across my face and opened the door. From behind his back, he revealed a giant pizza box.

"Oh my god! You didn't!" I squealed.

"I did!" he chuckled.

"You are amazing! Thank you!" I leaned up and kissed him. He leaned into the kiss, and I dragged him into the room.

"Wanna eat this in bed?" he asked gleefully.

"Yes, I do," I said. "I really do!"

He set the pizza down on the table and unbuttoned his work shirt.

"Do you mind if I make myself comfortable?" he asked.

I shook my head. "I don't mind at all." I walked over to him and ran my hands along his torso. I felt his hard muscles with my fingers. He was so unbelievably sexy. "How long do you think that pizza will stay warm for?" I leaned up again and pressed my lips into his. I bit down slightly on his bottom lip, and he inhaled deeply. I heard the beginnings of a growl coming from his chest.

"Maybe ten to fifteen minutes," he said softly, his lips still close to mine. He put his hands around my waist and pulled me into him.

"Perfect," I said. "You know, I've never minded cold pizza."

"Some say it's even better," he said. He lifted me off the ground and carried me straight to the bed.

A little while later we sat on my bed in the hotel robes, and I sunk my teeth into my first slice of pizza since I left the U.S. I nearly moaned. I was so hungry, and it was so good. I didn't care one bit that it was room temperature.

Gio sat cross-legged, facing me, his foot resting against my foot. "Today was a tough day, wasn't it?" he asked.

"It was," I agreed, in between chews. "Tomas and his team are really rude. I didn't realize this would be such a difficult project."

"They are tough," he agreed. "I am going to sit down with Charles and Jake tomorrow and discuss a strategy with them. I don't think these in person meetings are working. Tomas really hates Lola and it's making it hard to get anything done."

I took another bite of pizza and multiple thoughts swirled around in my head as I chewed. "Should I be concerned?" I asked. "I thought having you around was just a precaution...but now I'm starting to worry."

"Tomas is all talk," he assured me "When I worked for Grupo Merced, he never asked me to actually hurt anyone."

"Really?" I felt a huge amount of relief.

"He wanted me to intimidate people and scare them. I don't know if he's changed, but that's how he was when I knew him."

"So, you think we're still okay with the merger?" I asked.

"Si." He nodded at me. "At the end of the day, it's still in Tomas' best interest to finish the merger so he can move on with whatever he's doing." He tossed his pizza crust back into the box.

"So, we're not in danger?" I asked.

"No," he smiled at me. "You are not in danger, Bella...Well, maybe in danger of getting little sleep tonight."

I giggled and tossed my pizza crust in the box. "Is that so?"

"Yes," He grinned. "It is so."

I licked my fingers clean and then moved closer to him. I wrapped my legs around his waist, so I was practically in his lap. "Sleep is overrated." I said kissing him as I undid his robe. It was clear we were not going to be getting any sleep tonight.

CHAPTER EIGHTEEN
El Regreso de la Niña

The next day we arrived at the office and George had transformed our conference room to look like a game show studio. The TV was projecting what looked like a jeopardy board with the following categories across the top: Team Personalities and Facts, Mexico History, Client History, and Global Core facts. On the white board there was a scoreboard with pre-determined teams. The red team was Jake, Lola, Ricardo, and me. The blue team Charles, Chela, Gio, and Max. George immediately went into game host mode.

"Welcome to Global Core Jeopardy!" he said. "An interactive way to see who knows our team and clients the best. Please sit with your respective teams."

"¿Que es esto?" Chela asked Ricardo.

"Forced office fun," Jake scoffed before Ricardo could respond.

"Ooo, I'm excited," I said immediately taking my seat next to Ricardo.

Charles looked at the team. "I asked George to put together an activity for us to bring the team together. It's been a long couple of days."

"We couldn't just go to a bar?" Ricardo asked.

"We can go to the bar later," Charles responded.

"Alright red team, you can go first, pick a category and a dollar value," George said, ignoring the cynicism. No one said anything. Lola and Jake were sulking with their arms crossed not wanting to engage.

I turned to Ricardo. "Should we select team personalities for 500?"

"¿Porque no?" Ricardo responded.

"Okay, team personalities for 500," I said.

"Great choice, Blake!" George said. "The question is... who is the most stubborn person on the team?"

"What is this a roast?" Jake asked.

Both teams huddled to select their answer. I wasn't sure what to say as it was clearly Jake or Lola, and I didn't want to offend either of them.

"We'll need an answer," George said.

Jake broke the ice, arms still crossed. "Well, clearly it's me or Lola."

"Problamenete it's me," Lola responded.

The team nodded in agreement, and I responded, "Who is Lola?"

"Wrong!" George shouted.

"What?!" We responded in unison.

"Who is Jake and Lola!" George replied gleefully.

"Hang on!" I exclaimed. "You said who *is* the most stubborn, not who *are* the most stubborn!"

"Okay blue team, your turn." George ignored me. I gave him a look and he raised his hands in mock-defense.

The Blue team huddled. "Team Personalities and facts for 400," Max said.

"Name the person on the team who knows how to surf."

"I'm guessing la rubia de California..." Ricardo gripped.

"Who is Blake!" Max exclaimed.

"Okay, I feel like you're making an assumption based on my hair color and where I'm from!" I said laughing. "But yes, I do surf."

"Correct! The blue team is on the board." The team cheered and high fived. This continued for nearly an hour and by the end of it, everyone seemed to be in good spirits.

As the game ended, George became more sincere. "It doesn't matter who wins the game, but what matters is that we operate as a team. If we disagree, we have a conversation and come to a mutually agreed upon solution."

"I want to apologize for the way I spoke to you, Lola," Jake said. "That was uncalled for. You've been the only one of us brave enough to go toe to toe with Tomas. I could probably learn a thing or two from you."

"Gracias, Jake," she said. "I'm sorry for the way I spoke to you too."

George looked like he was about to burst into tears of joy.

After a few days, Charles received a call from Carlos requesting that we attempt one last TSA meeting with Grupo Merced. Tomas had been sent the first portion of the paperwork and he seemed pleased. He was even offering to come to our offices. While Carlos seemed optimistic that this was a good sign, I was unsure, and it seemed like my team felt the same way. Everyone was up to their usual nervous habits in the minutes before Tomas arrived. Ricardo was sweating, George was humming...even Charles, who was usually stoic, kept checking his watch and pacing around the conference room.

"Lola, do you think maybe you should sit this one out?" Charles asked. He sounded pained.

"What?" Jake asked.

"Charles no, I need to be there," she said. "We can't let him think he's won, or he'll just keep trying to push and push."

"It might be better if we show him that we are a united front and he doesn't get to dictate the terms of our meetings," Jake offered.

"Alright," Charles said. "But let's just stay on task, okay?"

Lola nodded.

I could feel my shoulders tensing as Tomas and his team entered the room. He was so calm that it made me even more nervous. He smiled pleasantly at us as he sat down.

"Hola, todos," he said.

Everyone mumbled their hellos. My palms were sweating. I glanced over at Max. He looked nervous too.

"Hola," Jake said. "I won't waste anyone's time. We will begin with discussing the financial accounting TSA." He opened his laptop and shared his screen on the projector. There on the screen was the PowerPoint presentation that Chela and I had worked so hard on. "Okay, this data was aligned with the Timbre and Grupo Merced teams. Sam and our team have compiled the key data points for you."

I watched Tomas' face as he read through the slide. His calm demeanor faded immediately, and he looked irate.

Max looked at me and his eyes got wide.

"No!" Tomas spat out. "This information is false! We have at least double the amount of people doing accounting for Timbre. Are you trying to cheat us out of our money?!"

Jake looked to me. "Blake and Chela ran point on this session, so I'll let them speak to that point."

I froze in horror. I had prepared the presentation and the numbers were correct, but never in a million years had I expected to have to speak to it in this meeting. I cleared my throat and saw Gio in the back of the room giving me a nod of encouragement.

"Si," I began in Spanish. "As Jake mentioned, we aligned all the numbers with the Timbre and Grupo Merced teams. The Grupo Merced team made it very clear that there was not much work left for them to complete on behalf of Timbre—"

"I don't believe you, rubia!" Tomas cut me off. "This is insanity! Why must I sit here and listen to all these idiot women! Do you even know how to do business?!"

"Blake is being polite." Lola's voice cut through the room and silenced Tomas. "Your man, Sam, was telling your team that Grupo Merced should not be doing any work on behalf of Timbre. I am sure because of this and his presence in the room, they did not feel comfortable providing an accurate number. If that is not the correct number, we will update it appropriately, but this information is coming from *your* team, not ours."

A deeply uncomfortable silence spread through the room. I looked over to Sam, his little snake-like face looked like he'd smelled something rotten.

"Sam," Tomas whispered. "*¿Es verdad? Is this true?*"

"No, no señor," Sam protested. "Their team was deceiving in the way they presented the information. I told our team we needed to ensure there were no costs incurred for Grupo Merced, not that they shouldn't highlight all of the people doing work."

"That is false," Lola said again. "Sam is lying to you."

"Lola..." Charles had a slight edge to his voice.

"You have tested my patience for the last time, niña," Tomas said to Lola, his jaw clenched. "You better hope Gio is around to keep an eye on you."

"Hey!" Charles shouted. "That's enough, Tomas."

"C'mon man! That's messed up!" Max chimed in too.

"¡Tomas! ¡Para!" Ricardo looked livid.

It was clear that the patience of our team had run out too. Tomas was explicitly threatening Lola now and none of us were going to let that slide.

Lola stared at Tomas. "You don't know what I'm made of."

"Nothing I can't break," Tomas spat back.

"Tomas!" I heard Gio's voice from the back of the room as he walked towards him. "Enough with the threats. You chose to sell this division of Grupo Merced. Lola is doing her job. This team is doing their jobs."

"Stick to the terms you agreed to," Lola said slyly. "You're embarrassing yourself, hombre."

"Enough!" Tomas roared. "¡Vamanos!" Tomas stormed out of the room, with his team following suit.

I looked around the room and then turned to Lola. Her chest was heaving. She was furious.

"I'm sorry," she said to Charles.

"Don't be sorry," Charles said as he walked over and put a hand on her shoulder. "Fuck that guy."

We left the meeting unsure of what else we could do. "Should we go back to the office and try to prepare a rebuttal?" Jake asked.

"No," Charles said. "We've done enough for today. This is obviously going to be a huge roadblock for this deal. I'll call Carlos in the morning. For now, I think we should all go eat and try to forget about this meeting."

"What do you think Carlos will say?" Jake asked.

"Carlos has a bigger problem on his hands than we thought," Charles said.

"Maybe a team dinner would be a good idea," George offered. "I think we could all use a drink."

"Gio?" Jake asked. "Do you think Tomas is serious? Should we be concerned?"

"I've known Tomas for a long time, and he's never hurt anyone," Gio said. "He likes to intimidate, but he's not violent."

"Is it a bad idea to go out to dinner?" Charles asked.

"Let me make a call," Gio said. "I know a little place in Roma. The owner is a friend. It's far enough away from the office and the hotel, I think it should be okay there."

We arrived at Gio's friend's restaurant and were greeted by the owner, Simon.

"Hola, todos," he said. "We have a perfect table for you in our courtyard."

"Gracias Simon," Gio said.

"You will enjoy," Simon said. "There's a band that will be playing soon."

We smiled and nodded at Simon and then followed him out onto the patio. It was lush and green, with hanging plants everywhere. There was a small fountain in the corner and on the far end of the courtyard there was a small stage set up for the band.

We sat down and the hostess brought us menus, and the bussers brought us bottles of water. I poured myself a glass of water and took a sip. As the water hit my lips, I realized how hungry I was and then I realized how tired I was. I looked around the table and everyone's energy seemed low. Chela yawned.

"Well, that was quite the day," Ricardo lamented.

"Si," Chela said. "Que problemas."

George seemed determined to lift our spirits. "Don't worry, everyone," he said. "We are going to get through this."

"I dunno, man," Max lamented. "It feels like we're getting our asses handed to us in these meetings."

There were several groans of agreement around the table. Lots of slumped shoulders, lots of tired people sipping water.

"I know we got dealt a blow today," Charles said. "And I know we may have some problems with this deal now, but I'm still very proud of each and every one of you."

"Is he 'bout to give a speech?" Max asked.

"I think so," Jake responded.

"Lola... you have showed such gumption and have stood up for the client," Charles began.

"There it is," said Jake.

"Like clockwork," Max laughed.

Charles smiled and ignored them. "George, Jake, so much leadership. It seems most likely that you'll both have to share my job when I retire." Jake and George cracked a smile. "Max, Ricardo, you're handling so much of the technical content, it's impressive. Chela, Blake, your care and attention to detail has really saved us with these TSAs. Gio, you've kept our team feeling safe and confident in the face of a lot of drama."

"And you've been a great tour guide for some of us," Max said with a wink.

I rolled my eyes at him playfully.

"We've become quite the little familia," Charles said, "And I am so proud to go into battle with you all."

My face pulled up into a smile. Charles was right. We were a family, and we had all grown to love and care for each other. In that instant there was a part of me that never wanted the merger to be finalized, because then our time together would be over. Even though we'd had a tough week, the simple truth was that it was going to be very hard to leave when the deal was done.

At that moment a pitcher of margaritas came to the table, and we filled our glasses.

"Compliments of Simon," said one of the servers.

"Gracias," Gio said.

"To family!" George said as he raised his glass.

"To family!" We all chimed in.

A couple pitchers of margaritas, and several plates of tacos later, we were feeling much better. Everyone was chatting animatedly around the table as we'd become so accustomed to doing when we were out together. Gio and I were sitting next to each other, and he even placed his hand on my thigh under the table. It was thrilling.

As our dinner wound down, the band started playing and as the music filled the restaurant, I started to feel my shoulders bobbing along.

"I think someone wants to dance," Chela said gesturing toward me.

I laughed. "I just love live music!"

"Gio, take her for a spin on the dance floor," Lola said.

I wasn't sure what to say. I had no idea what Charles, or George or Jake knew. "Oh! I can just—"

Gio glanced around the room, I assumed to make sure it was safe to leave the table for a bit.

"The jig is up, Blake," George laughed. He waved me off. "Go have fun!"

Gio stood up and took my hand. He led me out to the dance floor.

"Go have fun you love birds!" Max called after us.

"Ay ay ay!" Chela called from the table.

The music filled the restaurant and the tequila warmed up my blood. I pulled my hair out of its top knot and finally let myself cut lose with Gio's hands resting against my back. He spun me around the restaurant as the music played and I felt completely invigorated. Now that it seemed our team knew about us, I felt like we could just act like a normal couple in public.

Couple? I wondered. *Are we a couple?* The music slowed and he pulled me close to him. I leaned into his embrace and his fingers caressed my back as we danced. My mind became flooded with a supercut of all the moments we'd had together since we met. And as the memories flooded my mind, I tried to savor each and every one of them, because I knew at that some point, I'd have to go back to Dallas, and then I might never see him again.

"You look beautiful tonight," he said into my ear. "I can't stop thinking about you."

I looked up at him and our eyes locked. Something in the middle of my heart began to hurt. "I don't want to leave," I said, without thinking.

"¿Qué?" he asked.

"I just keep thinking that we're going to finish this deal soon and then..." I didn't want to finish my sentence. Because the words I was about to say were too sad.

"We will figure it out, bella," he said to me.

"Will we?" I asked.

"Don't worry we can—" the song changed, and the music got loud and fast again. Before Gio could finish his sentence, Ricardo and Chela were on the dance floor. Then Max followed suit.

"Having fun?" Ricardo asked us as he spun Chela around.

Gio just smiled at them. "Si," he said. He spun me around and we continued dancing. He gave me a look that said, *we can talk later don't worry*, so I just nodded, and we kept dancing.

The music continued. Max, Ricardo, and Chela stayed on the dance floor with us. Jake was talking to a woman at the bar and when I glanced at the table, I saw George, Lola and Charles talking. Everyone seemed to be having fun. Periodically I watched Gio clocking all of our team members to make sure that everyone was accounted for.

After a while, the band announced they'd be taking a break and there was a huge rush of people going to the bar, to the restroom, and back to their tables. We all returned to the table for water and another round of drinks. Gio and I plopped back into our seats, and I reached for the water pitcher.

Ricardo filled his margarita glass. "We need to raise a toast to our jefa fuerte, Lola!" he said.

"Si!" I agreed.

We all raised our glasses, but quickly noticed that Lola wasn't at the table.

"Where is Lola?" I asked.

"She was just here," Charles said. We all looked around the restaurant, but she was nowhere to be seen.

"I just saw her sitting with you two," Jake said to George and Charles. "Where did she go?"

"Did she say she was going to the restroom?" Ricardo asked. "I thought I saw her get up."

"Her purse is still here," I pointed out. "She must be in the restroom."

"I was just in there," Chela said. "I didn't see her."

I looked at Gio, he looked worried all of a sudden. "We'll go check," he said, gesturing for me to join him. We got up from the table and hurried to the restroom.

There was a line forming, but I moved past the women waiting and knocked on the door. "Lola? Are you in there?" I called. A couple of giggling girls in short dresses walked out of the restroom stumbling over each other, but I didn't see anyone else.

I walked inside. "Lola! ¿Estás aquí?"

"Lola!" I heard Gio call.

"She's not there," I said. I felt immediately sober as panic began to take hold of me.

Gio started asking the women in the line if they'd seen anything suspicious, but no one had anything helpful to say. I looked around, making sure we hadn't somehow missed Lola in the group, and then I saw it.

"Gio look," I said. The back gate to the courtyard was wide open. Behind it there was a dark alleyway. For a moment my brain wouldn't let me comprehend it. *Would someone really have followed us here?* Before I could finish my thought, a door opened partway down the alley. It looked like the restaurant's kitchen. One of the cooks walked outside and turned on a light. As the light flooded the space, something on the ground caught my eye. I walked over to it and picked it up.

"¿Que es?" Gio asked.

I held it up and showed Gio. "It's a lipstick."

"Shit," Gio said. "C'mon."

We ran back to the table. Everyone was looking slightly confused. "Did you find her?" George asked.

"No," I said. I looked at Gio. He looked sick with panic. I felt immediately guilty. I'd distracted him all night. "But we found this near the bathroom." I held up the lipstick.

"That looks like hers," Chela said.

"Maybe she's just outside on a call?" Ricardo asked. There was an edge to his voice.

Chela picked up Lola's purse and opened it. She reached in and held up Lola's phone. Her keys were in there too.

"Call the police," Gio instructed Ricardo.

I sat down in my chair with a thud, my body frozen in horror. Lola was gone.

CHAPTER NINETEEN
La Desparacida

The moments immediately following Lola's disappearance were a complete and total blur. Gio turned stone cold but then almost immediately sprang into action, barking orders at everyone and moving swiftly to ensure we were all safe.

I heard him on his phone asking for extra security to take Chela and Ricardo home and guard their homes until further notice.

Chela's face had gone ash white. She looked very shaken. Ricardo was trying to comfort her, and I walked over and gave her hand a squeeze.

"We'll find her," I said. "Don't worry." I wasn't sure what was giving me such confidence, but I had faith in Gio.

The police arrived and sat us all down. There were three of them. They looked like military officers with large guns, knee high combat boots and fresh pressed uniforms. I had seen federalis in other parts of Mexico but never up close. They were aggressive and shuffled us to a private place to speak. Two of them had notepads and were taking notes as we spoke. Most of the questions were addressed to those in our group who spoke Spanish. The lead officer addressed us with the questions.

"When was the last time you saw her?" he asked.

"About an hour ago," Jake answered.

"Did she say anything about where she was going?" he asked.

We all shook our heads. "Her purse is still here, and her phone is inside," Chela said, holding it up to show the police.

"We will need to take that into evidence," one of the officers said.

"Is that necessary?" Ricardo asked. "How will she get it back?"

"We will handle it," the lead officer said. "Was she drinking a lot?"

"What? No!" Ricardo sounded defensive.

"Lo siento. We have to ask," the officer said. "Did she have any enemies that you know of? Anyone who might like to see her hurt?"

We all looked at each other. "We had a rather tense business meeting today," Jake allowed. "But our security does not believe these men are violent."

"What about Sam?" I chimed in. "He's been causing trouble since the beginning. And he's been stalking me. Every time I go out with Gio, he's there. Are we sure he didn't do this?"

"Who is Sam?" the officer asked.

Before I could answer, Jake jumped in. "He's been stalking you?"

"Sam Garcia," Gio stepped in. "He's a liaison between our team and Grupo Merced."

The officer stopped Gio. "Grupo Merced? La compania de Tomas Barajas?"

Gio, not missing a beat, responded "It's his job to try and keep our team on the defensive and make them feel unsettled so that they're not as tough in the negotiations. I don't believe he'd do anything. I used to work for him. He likes to scare people but never saw him hurt anyone."

"And yet one of your friends has gone missing," the officer said.

"Why not check out Sam?" I asked Gio. "You've noticed him following us around."

"Sam wouldn't do this," he said.

"Why is he always following us then?" I asked in disbelief. *Was he really defending Sam?* "I've seen him numerous times."

Out of the corner of my eye I saw the officers whispering to each other likely determining next steps.

"Polanco is a small area, and he lives there," Gio explained to the officers. "Otherwise, we've only seen him at the office and in meetings."

My stomach was in knots. There was something off about the way Gio was handling this and I wanted to speak up again, but for some reason I decided I'd rather talk to him in private.

"Alright," the officer said. "I think we have everything we need. We're going to do a search in the area, but you should all go home for now. We'll let you know if we find anything."

If? My stomach tightened. *Why not when?*

"Gio, do you think she's actually been kidnapped?" Max asked.

"I don't know," Gio said. "I need to make some calls."

"This is crazy," Max said.

"It just feels way too coincidental that this would happen right after the meeting today," George said.

"I was worried about a team dinner," Charles said. "We should have eaten at the hotel."

As we arrived back at the hotel, I wanted nothing more than for Gio to come up to my room so we could talk, but he dropped us off at the carport and his colleague was waiting to walk us in. I felt frustrated that I couldn't have him to myself to find out what he thought was going on and why he had defended Sam.

"Can we talk? I asked.

"Not right now. I need to make some calls, Blake," he said. His brow furrowed.

"Okay," I answered.

His colleague walked us all into the hotel and I saw Gio drive away.

As I walked into my room, I felt completely numb and exhausted. I kept checking my phone thinking maybe I'd hear some news, but there was nothing. I locked and bolted the door and then sat on the bed, trying to come to terms with my current reality. I decided to tidy up my room. It didn't really matter because no one was going to see it, but it occupied my hands while my mind raced.

My phone buzzed and I jumped, praying it somehow was Lola and the nightmare was over.

"Don't open the door for anyone tonight." It was Gio. "Not even the butler."

I responded and agreed I wouldn't open the door. I was about to type that what happened to Lola wasn't his fault, and ask why he didn't suspect Sam, but I didn't want to interrupt him further while he was working. "You're welcome to come back here and stay with me tonight," I texted.

He replied back, "I won't be sleeping tonight. I went to Lola's and no one is there, so I'm going to meet with Sam."

My stomach tightened again. I had so many questions. I wanted to know everything he was thinking but I knew I couldn't ask right now. *Was I right about Sam? Could he have possibly taken Lola? Or orchestrated this?* Max had been right that the timing was too coincidental. We all heard Tomas threaten Lola. I just never thought anything would come of it. He seemed like a bully, but not a criminal.

I texted him back. "Please let me know if you find out anything and stay safe."

I tried taking a hot bath to calm my nerves, but my brain wouldn't stop, and I was starting to feel like it was going to explode. I couldn't stop thinking about where Lola might be and if she was okay. I felt my feelings wavering between fear, anger, confusion, and resentment. By the time I was done with my bath I had decided. There was no coincidence here, this had to be Tomas' work. He had it out for Lola, and we all knew it. It was an insane idea to wrap my brain around because things like this just didn't happen in Dallas after a tough meeting. Once I allowed myself to believe it, I decided that I couldn't just sit idly by and do nothing.

I was lying in bed trying to sleep when my phone buzzed. I jumped up hoping it was Gio, but it was Max.

"Still awake? Any chance you want to meet up at the lobby bar for a drink?"

I thought twice about it. "Do you think it's safe?" I knew if Gio found out he would be upset but, I also didn't want to be alone and I was still a grown woman who had ownership over my own choices.

Max responded within seconds. "George and I are already here with a new security detail. Come on down"

"Okay, see you soon."

When I got down to the lobby bar, they already had a glass of wine waiting for me. The new security guard, Rafael sat at another table by the door, giving us some privacy.

Max had a notepad out with what looked like a bunch of gibberish scribbled on it. He started to tell me that he and George were trying to map out the restaurant and how someone could have taken Lola without us seeing. "We're trying to remember who was around us, and if any of them look like people from Grupo Merced," Max said in a hushed voice.

"Did you see anyone that looked familiar?" George asked.

"No," I admitted. "But..."

"But what?" Max asked.

I took a deep breath. "When Gio and I went to check the bathroom, we noticed that the back gate of the courtyard was open."

"What?" George said.

"And it opened onto a dark alleyway," I admitted.

"Shit..." Max sighed.

"So, are you saying you think someone from Grupo Merced followed us to the restaurant from our own offices and grabbed Lola while she was coming out of the bathroom?" George asked. "How would they have known we were even going to go out?"

"Sam has been following Gio and I for weeks," I admitted. "He showed up at one of the restaurants Gio took me on a date to."

"Why didn't you tell us this?" George seemed increasingly alarmed.

"Well, I didn't really want everyone to know about my personal life," I said.

"But Blake," Max began. "Just being real, your personal life got entangled with your work life when you started dating our security guard who has a history working with the dude who you're now saying has been stalking you! It might have been a good idea to tell us that."

"Okay, yeah that's pretty bad," I admitted.

"What is Gio's history with Sam?" George asked.

"I'm not really sure yet," I admitted. "Gio just said they worked together at Grupo Merced but that he left, and Sam didn't."

"And Sam knows y'all have been dating?" Max asked.

"Yes," I said.

"So, he might have known that Gio would be distracted if we were all out to dinner, now that you two are all up in each other's business."

"That's feasible, yes," I said. I didn't mention to them that Gio was probably meeting with Sam as we spoke.

"Okay we have to think about this logically," George said. "Obviously Lola pissed them off, but in the end, what do they want?"

"To be done with us," Max said. "I mean, the deal. Done with the deal."

"And it is in their best interest for that to go smoothly," George said. "I'd imagine they wouldn't want a lot of extra attention brought onto themselves."

"I don't know... Lola did embarrass Tomas more than once," I said. "I mean it was amazing! She kicked ass. But she and Chela told me that Mexican men are very prideful. I don't think he appreciated being called out by a woman."

"True. Especially if he has a certain... reputation to uphold." George responded.

"So, we agree they have to be a part of the cartels, right?" I asked in a hushed tone. "Like this company is a front. I know we haven't discussed this as a team, but it seems so obvious now."

"I don't want to make assumptions," George said. "But yes, Charles, Jake and I have discussed that Tomas is likely involved in other, more insidious businesses through Grupo Merced."

"How did we get mixed up in this George?" I asked. "Why the hell didn't Global Core do its due diligence here?"

"I should have stayed in L.A." Max lamented. "This shit is too crazy for me."

"Charles has been talking with corporate about our concerns," George said. "He didn't want to alarm anyone, but there's been some talk about us pulling out of the deal and handling it remotely from the states."

"Really?" I asked. "We're leaving?" My heart sank. Even if there was a real threat to our team, I couldn't possibly leave until we found Lola... and then there was Gio...

"Nothing has been decided," George said. "This discussion happened a few days ago. I have no idea how the Lola situation will affect us going forward."

"I don't feel right just getting on a plane with her missing," Max said.

"Neither do I," I agreed.

"Well, for now I think we have to trust Gio and the authorities to handle it," George said. "There's not much we can do ourselves."

It felt like we were talking in circles, and it was time for us to try and sleep. The security guard walked us all back to our rooms to make sure we got there safely. Once inside, I laid in bed, mind racing again, trying to remember every moment from the night until I must have drifted to sleep.

The next morning, my alarm hit me like a brick wall, I laid in bed numb, hoping that the night before was simply a bad dream. I laid there covering my eyes trying to will myself into a different reality. My phone buzzed again. This time it was a text from George to Max and me. "Corporate has suggested to Charles that we all go home," he said.

It wasn't long before Max's reply pinged through. "I'm not leaving until we find out what's happened with Lola."

I responded myself. "I'm with Max."

George responded again. "I agree," he said, "I'm glad we're aligned. We can tell Charles when we go in today."

I got dressed and out the door in a fog. So much was happening, and I hardly knew how to process it. When I got to the elevator, Max was standing waiting for the elevator down.

"No one left behind," he said.

I nodded. "No one left behind."

We rode down the elevator together to the lobby where we were met by Rafael.

"Buenas Dias," he said to us.

"Where is Gio?" I asked, trying to sound nonchalant.

"Occupied," Rafael said. Suddenly I started to worry about where Gio really was and what might have happened overnight with Sam.

George, Jake and Charles met us in the lobby shortly thereafter. "Good morning," Charles said in a somewhat somber tone.

"We're not going anywhere," Max said, beating Charles to the punch. "Lola is part of our Mexico City family. We're finding her."

"I agree entirely," Charles said. "Let's get to the office."

As we arrived at Timbre, Gio was walking into the office. I nearly gasped at the sight of him, I was so relieved. I looked at him intently, hoping he'd make eye contact with me, but he didn't.

We made our way to Carlos' office to find him looking disheveled. I couldn't help but wonder if he'd even slept.

Carlos looked at Gio. "Did you have any luck?"

"No," Gio said. "He didn't come home last night. I tried to call his cell and the office, but he's not there."

"Shit." Carlos looked panicked.

"So, what do we do?" Carlos asked. "Even if the police help it might take too long. Does this mean we have to try and find Lola ourselves?"

"No," Gio said firmly. "That is my job. You all need to stay together so no one else gets hurt."

"Well, maybe we can help in other ways then," Charles said. "Is there anything from our meetings with Grupo Merced that might point to where you can start looking? Anything Tomas or Sam might have mentioned?"

"Didn't you tell me that Timbre some old offices here in Mexico City?" I asked Charles. "What if she was taken there? Sam might have known about them."

"We can check there," Gio said. "Rafael, dile a Manuel que revise allí."

Rafael nodded, picked up his phone and left the room.

Ricardo, who looked as though he hadn't slept at all spoke up. "Well, Gio, where did you guys take people when you needed to get rid of a body?"

"Excuse me?" Gio sounded indignant.

"Where would you torture people?"

"Ricardo!" Chela scolded him.

"What!" Ricardo retorted. "We all know that Gio used to work for Tomas, and now we have seen firsthand what Tomas is capable of. So maybe Gio should go visit some of his old stomping grounds."

"I never tortured anyone," Gio said. "There is a difference between intimidation and violence."

"Ricardo, I think you should go home," Jake said. "This isn't helping."

"No!" Ricardo kept pushing. "Gio knows Tomas better than anyone else in this room. I'm asking him for information and he's holding out on us. I want to know where Lola is! ¡Tu sabes, Gio! You know where Lola is!"

"If I knew where Lola was, she wouldn't be there!" Gio shouted. "She would be here with us! You think I did this? I'm part of *this* team! I'm here to protect you!"

"Well, you did a good job of that last night." Ricardo's voice was cold. "Bien trabajo."

The whole room fell silent in shock and Gio just stood there looking like he'd been slapped in the face.

"You used to work for Tomas. You knew Sam. Maybe you were added to our team as a spy for Grupo Merced."

I couldn't take it anymore and I turned to Ricardo. "Enough—this isn't helping!"

"Blake is right," Max interjected. "We need everyone to work together to find Lola. We are all on the same team."

"Ricardo, I'm sorry but you need to go home and rest," said Jake. "I insist. Take the day."

"Puta madre!" Ricardo angrily gathered his things and made his way toward the door. "I know you know something, Gio," he said. His words sent a chill down my spine. Ricardo left the office and the door slammed behind him.

I turned to Gio and placed my hand on his and he brushed it away. He looked baffled and angry. "Gio—"

"Rafael will be with you today," he interrupted me. He sounded hollow. "I need to go and take care of a few things."

Without another word, Gio walked out of the room the same way Ricardo had, except the door didn't slam. He made sure to close it gently, almost as if he didn't want to cause any more damage.

CHAPTER TWENTY
La Búsqueda

After forty-eight hours, nothing had really changed. We had heard nothing from Lola, the police had nothing to report, and everyone continued to feel tense and worried. Chela had to contact Lola's family to let them know that she was missing, which was gut-wrenching to witness. I watched her walk back into our office after making the calls and her eyes were wet and bloodshot. She looked exhausted and hopeless.

By the end of the day, most of our team had already gone back to the hotel. Carlos, Gio, Jake, Ricardo and I stayed late to see if there was anything we'd missed. We combed through emails we'd received from both Sam and Tomas' office. Notes from our meetings, we searched online for articles about Tomas, and others on missing persons cases in the Mexico City area to see if there were any similarities, or anything to tip us off to Lola's whereabouts, but nothing added up. At one point the police called Gio's phone to let him know that they'd searched the city, and reviewed security camera footage in Polanco and Roma, but had found no trace of Lola. There was a tip line that people could call with information, but none of the calls they'd received led to anything concrete. They assumed it was just people trying to get reward money.

Finally, Carlos decided to call Tomas. We agreed that accusing him outright wouldn't help anyone. We wondered however if we made him aware of the situation if he'd say something that might tip us off.

Tomas' secretary put us through to him and when Tomas answered the phone, the whole room tensed up. "Tomas, we have a problem," Carlos said. "Our team member, Lola has gone missing we're wondering if anyone on your team has seen her." Carlos was impressive. I don't know how he managed to remain so cool and calm. It took every ounce of self-control I had not to start screaming at Tomas over the speakerphone.

Tomas laughed and I felt my blood pressure begin to rise. "I wonder who else she has disrespected recently," he said. "She really should have learned to watch her mouth by now."

Ricardo looked like he was ready to jump through the phone and beat the life out of Tomas.

"Don't," Jake whispered, barely audible.

"I have not seen her," Tomas said. "but, I'm sure there are plenty of other men who would like to see her out of the way." I reached down and grabbed Ricardo's hand and squeezed it. I knew we both wanted to scream, and it was difficult to remain silent while this awful man mocked the pain that he must have known we were all experiencing. He squeezed back. "Have you considered the ex-husband?" Tomas continued. "I heard she was a real ball-buster in their marriage. Poor guy was pushed around by her until they finally got divorced. Maybe he's out for vengeance."

We all looked at each other. *How the hell did Tomas know such personal details about Lola's life? And was there a real possibility that Tomas was innocent, and it was someone else in Lola's life who might have done this?*

I looked at Ricardo and whispered, "Should we go see the ex-husband?"

Gio overheard us and he shot back, "No, *we* do not need to go anywhere. *I* will go talk to the ex-husband."

Carlos reached down swiftly and muted the phone call. "If you all need to discuss something please go out in the hall."

"Come with me," Gio said taking my hand and pulling me out of the room while gesturing to Ricardo to join us as Carlos finished up with Tomas.

"You two are not going to run around this city trying to be heros. I need you to stay out of the way so we can work. Esto no es un juego. Esto es serio. This is a missing persons case."

Hearing Gio say missing person aloud I felt like I had the wind knocked out of me, I started to feel faint. Next thing I knew I was sitting down on the ground with Ricardo rubbing my back. Gio brought me a glass of water.

As he handed me the glass of water, Gio looked at me with calming eyes and asked, "Are you OK?" It was the most he had said to me directly since he dropped me off at the hotel two nights prior.

"I'm fine," I responded, even though I was nowhere close to fine.

Ricardo looked at me and then Gio, "Gio, we just want to help," he said. "Our friend is missing, and we feel useless sitting here in the office. Lola's ex-husband lives between here and the St. Regis. Let us help. Let us go talk to him with you. I've met him a few times. Maybe he will talk to me."

I wasn't clear if it was because Gio was tired or if he took pity on us, but he reluctantly agreed to escort us to Lola's ex-husband's apartment.

As we drove to the house, Gio explained that this was likely a distraction to keep us off of Tomas and Sam's trail, but Ricardo didn't seem as convinced.

"We don't know that, and at least we're doing something," he said.

"Do you think the husband could have something to do with this?" I asked Gio.

"The husband is always the first suspect," he said. "But it doesn't sound like they had a bad separation."

"Either way, we should talk to him." Ricardo said. I looked at Gio just in time to see him roll his eyes. Ricardo was clearly getting on his nerves, and it seemed obvious that the tension from the day before had not yet subsided.

When we arrived, Ricardo was the one to walk toward the door first and he knocked with purpose.

A tall man with dark slicked back hair answered.

"Hola, Mauricio," Ricardo said.

"Ricardo... qué sorpresa. ¿Que tal?"

Ricardo introduced Gio and me in Spanish and then explained why we were there to talk with him.

"Thank you for seeing us," Gio said to Mauricio.

"Of course," Mauricio said. "Please come in." We entered the house and he asked us to take a seat on the couch. He looked confused and concerned. "How long has she been gone for?" he asked. "I hadn't heard anything."

"One of our team members contacted her immediate family earlier today," I said. "I imagine if you're still in touch with any of them, they'll be calling you later."

"Are you here because you think I might have something to do with this?" Mauricio asked. "Because while my marriage to Lola didn't work out, there was never any kind of violence between us. And we haven't spoken in months" I watched his face to see if he looked suspicious or cagey as he spoke, but he didn't. He looked genuinely worried.

"It's just a precaution," Gio assured him. "In these kinds of cases, unfortunately the husband or ex-husband is always the first person to speak with. I'm surprised the police haven't reached out to you already."

"I've been out of town for the last couple of weeks," Mauricio said. "I just returned this morning and I'm happy to prove this. I was at a hotel in San Miguel de Allende with my girlfriend." He pulled out his phone to show us the reservation and receipts for the trip on his phone.

I looked at Gio. His teeth were set, and he looked like he was ready to go. "Thank you, Mauricio," he said. "We won't take any more of your time."

"Please let me know when you find her," he said.

"We will," said Ricardo. They shook hands.

I could feel the tension as we got back into the car. I knew Gio was frustrated that we'd wasted our time, but Ricardo seemed eager to prove that we hadn't.

"Well, okay now we know it wasn't him," Ricardo said.

"Ricardo, we have an entire team investigating this, why do you need to be part of this?" Gio asked.

"I just wanted to make sure it wasn't a lead," Ricardo said.

"It wasn't a lead, Ricardo!" Gio shot back. "It was a diversion left for us by Tomas and it was a waste of our time. Every hour counts right now. I am taking you both home and need you to stay there until the morning."

I heard Ricardo snort. "Gio, I'm not a child, I can go wherever I want."

"It would be easier if you didn't," he said. Gio picked up his phone and made a quick call. When the person on the other end answered all Gio said was, "Siegues adelante." *Go ahead.*

Gio and Ricardo didn't say another word to each other for the rest of the drive. I was hopeful that things would calm down between them, but when we got to Ricardo's home there was a security guard at the front door waiting for him.

"¿Quien es esto?" Ricardo asked, perturbed.

"Manuel can accompany you anywhere else you need to go this evening." Gio said with a condescending smile. "Not my choice. It's Global Core's."

"Puta Madre," Ricardo gargled under his breath as he got out of the car and slammed the door.

Gio sped through the city, weaving in and out of cars. I felt my heart rate quicken. It was the first time we'd been alone since the night Lola had disappeared and I longed for things to feel intimate and calm between us.

"Where are you going so fast?" I asked.

"I want to try to go see Sam again, I think I can convenience him to help us."

"Let me go with you. Maybe he'll say something that will trigger my memory."

"No, Blake. It's not safe."

"Please don't take me back to the hotel yet," I said. "I don't want to be all alone feeling helpless. Let me do something useful." I reached my hand over and placed it on the back of his neck. I massaged it ever so slightly. I could feel how tense he was and felt him relax a bit at my touch. "If you take me all the way back to the hotel and then have to circle back to his place, you'll lose time. Isn't his place on the way back to the hotel anyway?"

"How did you know that?" he asked.

"I didn't," I said. "Just a lucky guess."

Gio rolled his eyes, but eventually acquiesced. "Fine, but if you come with me, you have to do whatever I say. For your own good, okay?"

"Okay."

As we turned onto Sam's street, Gio slowed the car and turned off the headlights. Then he parked a few houses down so his truck wouldn't be visible from the windows.

"Stay in the car," he said to me.

I watched him exit the car and walk slowly and carefully up to Sam's front door. He walked along the side of the house so as not to be seen.

When he knocked on the door, he turned his back to the front door and waited. Eventually Sam opened the door and as soon as he did Gio grabbed him by the collar of his shirt and dragged him back into the house, slamming the door behind him.

There was a commotion from inside the house and then everything went silent. I had to know what was going on. Carefully I opened the door of Gio's truck and crept quietly up the lawn, standing behind a tree so they couldn't see me.

"What the hell, Sam!" Gio shouted. "We had a deal! And this wasn't part of it. Where is she?!" *A deal? What did he mean by that?*

"I don't know what you're talking about," Sam said. He was a bad actor. It was clear he knew exactly what Gio was talking about. Or he was intentionally mocking Gio, which didn't seem wise.

"You know exactly what I'm talking about!" Gio's voice was filled with anger. I'd never heard him so upset before. "Where is Lola?! ¿Donde está ella?"

"You knew what you signed up for," Sam spit back coldly at Gio.

"Taking her was never part of the agreement!" he shouted. "You double crossed me!" My heart sank at his words. *What agreement? Was Gio still working for Grupo Merced? Was Ricardo right about him?*

"Just like you double crossed your team." I saw Sam through the window finally. He gave Gio a look of disdain. I wanted to punch him. I wanted to hurt him, the same way he had hurt us. Gio moved out of my view and into another area of the room. I couldn't hear his words anymore and my heart was beginning to race. I felt my stomach twist into a sickening knot. "Please, no." I whispered quietly. I didn't want Ricardo to be right.

Sam walked back into my view. "You know what you have to do then," Sam said to Gio. "You have no choice."

"I can't..." I heard Gio say.

"It's the only way..."

"Is this about Mateo?" Gio asked.

I felt my body tense at this. I tried to decipher what they were talking about, but it was hard to put specific meaning to the words. I stepped forward to try and hear better but instead I heard the sharp *crack!* as a twig snapped beneath my shoe. *Shit.*

Sam's eyes shot toward the window. I tried to move out of his view and back behind the tree, but it was too late. He walked to the window and opened it.

"Well, look what we have here," he said. "A little spy. She's learned from the best."

"Sam, shut up. Blake! What are you doing? I told you to stay in the car!"

"I—" I stammered, but I didn't know what else to say. My head was spinning. All at once I wanted to be as far away from him as possible. And at the same time, I wanted nothing Sam had just said to be true.

"Goddammit! Why didn't you listen to me?!" His words were like ice. "If you and Lola would have just listened maybe none of this would have ever happened!"

Words failed. I opened my mouth to speak, but no sound came out. I looked at Gio's face. He looked like a different person. Like someone I'd never known at all. I pulled out my phone to call an Uber, but the closest car was thirty minutes away. Instead, I shared my location with Max and George and sent them a quick text to tell them what was going on.

"Max and George know where I am and they know what's going on," I said to Gio. "I would like you to take me back to the hotel now."

He growled. "Sam, don't you dare go anywhere. We're nowhere near finished here."

CHAPTER TWENTY-ONE
El Colapso

As we drove back to the hotel, I vacillated between wanting to scream in rage and burst into tears. I wanted answers. I wanted to know what Sam meant. I wanted him to tell me that I'd heard it wrong. That I'd misunderstood. I wanted him to set the record straight. Gio had kept us safe the entire time we'd been in Mexico City. How could we have been so wrong about him?

"What did Sam mean?" I demanded. "Why did he call you a spy?"

"We're not talking about that now."

"The hell, we are!" I shot back. "I've been asking you about Sam for weeks! And you kept dodging the question. I'm not an idiot, Gio. Stop treating me like one! Tell me the truth."

"Sam now knows that *you* know that we spoke. That complicates things for me."

"You're dodging the question," I shot back. "Tell me what is your relationship with Sam? Why do you keep defending him? Why did he call you a spy? Are you working with Grupo Merced? And who the hell is Mateo?!"

"Blake..." he trailed off.

"Answer me," I demanded. "Answer my questions now."

He took a breath. I watched his hands clench on the steering wheel. "Sam is like a brother to me," he said. "He was my best friend growing up and his family needed help just like mine did.

He came with me to work for Tomas. I left, but he didn't get out and now he might be tied up in something bad with Tomas' brother Mateo. I feel responsible because I led him to that life! I'm trying to get him out, and I'm trying to get him to tell me where Lola is."

"And what did he mean by, *you know what you have to do*?"

"What do you think?" he said.

"Are you still working for Tomas?" I asked.

"No," he said calmly. He took a deep breath. "But they want me to come back."

"No," I said horrified. "We can figure out another way."

"It's the only way," he said. "Sam says if I come back to work for Tomas, then we'll find out where Lola is."

"This isn't your fault."

"It *is* my fault!" he burst out. "It's my fault, Blake. It's my job to keep the team out of harm's way and now Lola is gone. If I had been paying more attention, if I hadn't gotten so wrapped up in *you*, this never would have happened!"

I felt the hot sting of rejection and shame at his words, and I felt myself go numb. *Was that true? Was it my fault that Lola was gone?*

"I—"

"Fuck Blake. I'm sorry." He sighed. "I didn't mean that. Of course, this isn't your fault."

"I feel like I don't even know you anymore," I said, choking back tears and turning my head towards the window so he couldn't see my face. In that instant I felt every positive, buoyant emotion I had felt surrounding Gio disappear into thin air. We pulled into the hotel valet, and I got out of the car. Gio didn't move from his seat. "I'll just show myself in then," I said numbly. "Hopefully I don't get kidnapped while you're wrapped up in Sam."

"Blake, please."

"Bye, Gio." I slammed the truck door and walked inside the hotel. Max and George were waiting for me in the lobby. As soon as I walked in the door, they rushed to my side. I saw the headlights of Gio's truck move away from the building.

"What happened?" George demanded. "Are you okay?"

"I'm fine," I answered. "Where's Charles?"

"Asleep I think," Max said.

"He called a meeting first thing in the morning," George said.

"Good," I said. "We all need to talk."

When we arrived at the office the next morning, Charles asked everyone to sit for a few announcements. No one had seen Gio all morning, but I was still so angry I hardly had time to care. Rafael and Manuel were with us, now.

"Carlos will be coming in this morning and we're going to have a meeting about the status of the merger," Charles said.

"What about Lola? Have we heard anything from Tomas?" I asked. I wanted to know everything that was going on with the case before I shared what I'd learned.

George and Max were eyeing me curiously, still intent on knowing what I'd learned the night before.

"We'll discuss that when Carlos gets here," Charles said. "Just sit tight for a few minutes and then we'll fill everyone in."

Chela was seated beside me. "What's going on?" she whispered. "What do you know?"

"What do you mean?" I asked.

"You just look like you know something," she said. "And where's Gio?"

"Come with me to the bathroom," I said, and we got up and walked out of the conference room and into the hall. "Gio went to talk to Sam last night and now he's not here."

"What? How do you know?"

"I was with him. But then we got in a fight, and he brought me back to the hotel. He told Sam he was coming back, and Sam saw me with him. It sounded like Sam knew something about Lola."

"You have to tell everyone," she said

"I know," I said. "I'm planning to. I just want to hear what they know first... and also I—" I stopped myself.

"Also, what?" she begged.

I hesitated as emotion overtook me. "It's Gio."

"What do you mean?"

"When he was at Sam's he said something to Sam about Lola's disappearance not being part of their deal, and Sam told Gio that Gio knows what he has to do to get Lola back."

"Ay que no! ¿Es un rata?"

"No sé. Sam told Gio he wanted him to come back to Grupo Merced in exchange for Lola, but I keep wondering what if it's a trick. What if something... bad has happened to Lola and they're just trying to play Gio to get him to agree to come back. What if they hurt him too?'

"We have to talk to Charles," Chela said, desperately. "We have to tell the team!"

"I know, you're right..." I fought back my tears. "I'm just scared. I want Lola to be safe, I don't want Gio to go back to working for Tomas. I'm just scared."

She hugged me. "I know, mija," she said. "But you have to be brave! I overheard Charles on the phone with Carlos. They're about to pull the plug on the merger and send you all home. Carlos said they will let the police handle finding Lola."

"What?" I gasped. "But will the police even be able to help? They haven't done anything so far!"

"And we don't know if they've been corrupted by the cartels," she said. "If you know something, something that could help Lola, we have to tell the team now!"

I took a deep breath. "Okay."

CHAPTER TWENTY-TWO
El Plan

Once Carlos had arrived, Charles sat everyone down and told us gravely, "As you probably all know by now, corporate wants to send you all home."

"Absolutely not," Jake said.

"I'm with Jake," Max said.

"I agree with your sentiment," Charles said. "And I respect it, but Global Core wants you all home."

"We can handle the rest of the deal ourselves," Carlos said. "It won't go as smoothly but we can figure it out. The police will handle the investigation and that's all we can do."

"No." George was firm. "Charles, I know you're just the messenger here, but we're not leaving."

I looked at Chela and she raised her hand. "Excuse me, Charles..."

"Yes, Chela," he said. "Blake has some information that might help."

Everyone turned their eyes toward me, and I felt my stomach do somersaults. "Yes, well..."

"Go ahead, Blake," Charles said.

I eyed him and then eyed Carlos. "Can we have the room?" I asked.

He understood. "Carlos, we'll fill you in later," Charles said. "Manuel will show you out."

"Gracias," Carlos said. He and Manuel walked out of the room. I had a feeling he wanted to hear what I had to say, but I was already uneasy enough about betraying Gio's trust even amongst our own team, so he'd have to wait.

"Jake, close the door behind him," Charles instructed.

"Alright." Jake got up and shut the door.

"Okay, Blake we're listening," Charles said calmly.

I took a deep inhale, steadied myself and spoke. "I think I might know who took Lola. Like, I think I might be able to confirm it."

I watched as dumbfounded expressions hit their faces and then I told them everything I knew. I told them about Gio and my relationship, which of course they now knew about. I told them about the interactions I'd witnessed with he and Sam, which of course was news to everyone in the room except for George and Max. I told them about what I'd seen last night and how Gio had gotten upset when I wanted more information, how he had defended Sam. I recounted the conversation I'd heard between them word for word, but this still left us at an impasse, because no one had heard from Gio, and Manuel had been unwilling or unable to help us find him.

"We have to call the police!" Charles said.

"We can't," Chela said.

"What? Why?" Charles asked.

"I think we all need to admit it," Jake said. "Tomas is in bed with the cartels, if not in one of them himself."

"If we go to the police, they might not help," said Ricardo, "And we put ourselves in more danger. The police are likely corrupt."

"Can we trust Gio to get her back?" Charles asked me.

"I... I don't know," I answered honestly. "Something has changed. Tomas wants Gio working for him again at Grupo

Merced. It's like he's taken it personally that Gio left. On top of that he clearly wants us to stop pushing with the merger. Lola is his bargaining chip."

"Dear lord, how did we get mixed up in this..." Charles lamented.

"This is crazy. If we give up the TSA discussions, we leave our clients in a lurch and our company," Max said.

"But if we don't, we're throwing Lola to the wolves," Ricardo countered.

"We're not letting Lola be the sacrificial pawn here. There has to be a way we can work this out," Charles said.

"I'm not sure how," Jake lamented. "We can't get in touch with Gio. We already told Tomas that she's missing, and he hasn't said anything helpful. And on top of that we still have a contractual obligation to PacSouth."

"Okay, here's what we're going to do." Charles lowered his voice. "No one says a word to corporate beyond what they already know. I'll give them a call and tell them that there seems to have been a misunderstanding and we're moving forward. Let's try to get all of our ducks in a row with the TSA's so we're prepared to close out the deal when Lola is back."

"What if she doesn't—" Chela began.

"I'm not allowing that thought in yet," Charles said defiantly. "If Lola and Gio have not returned in another day or so, then we will reconvene and discuss our options."

"Alright." Jake nodded.

"For now, I want everyone back at the hotel, that includes Ricardo and Chela and her daughter. Blake, can you talk to customer relations and see about getting us two more rooms? We'll put it on my personal card so as not to raise any flags."

"Okay," I said.

"I will chat with Jake and George, and we will send you each remote assignments to work on at the hotel. They have conference rooms there we can use, but for now, I don't want anyone near any Global Core, Timbre or Grupo Merced office. Got it?"

We agreed. Within the hour, we had cleared out of our office space and had packed up everything we would need to move our operations entirely over to the St. Regis.

I was able to connect with guest relations and they were able to get Chela and Ricardo rooms. They were also able to reserve one of the large conference rooms for us indefinitely.

It made me feel better to be able to do something, but there was still a lingering sense of dread even as we continued to push forward with our preparation for the next round of TSA negotiations. Everything with the merger was now hinging on Lola's return... and Lola's return was most likely hinging on Gio cutting some kind of deal with Sam and Tomas.

As the hours passed, and there was no sign of Gio or Lola, morale started to drop. The lively and collaborative energy we'd gotten used to had disappeared. Instead, it felt like we were just machines, diligently doing our work, without any kind of human connection.

The minutes and hours began to blend together as we did as much work as we possibly could to finalize the TSA paperwork from our hotel. We were subsisting solely on coffee and room service. Per Charles' plan to not have corporate interfere until Lola was found, we ate all of our meals at the hotel, and we never left the property. In his mind, we had no idea if Tomas had it out for any of the rest of us and it was better not to chance it.

As we began to finalize all of the TSA documents, it was a strange feeling. It seemed like spirits should be high, that we should be celebrating our accomplishment, but there was nothing to celebrate as long as Lola and Gio were missing. Sometimes we worked with the team in the conference room, sometimes we worked separately from our own hotel rooms.

No matter how bleak the circumstance was looking, I didn't want to leave Mexico until we found Lola. As for Gio, I was so upset and hurt by him that I forced myself to become numb to my feelings for him. He had chosen the path he was on now, Lola had not. I became singularly focused on completing the job so that once Lola was back safe, we would be done with Tomas as quickly as possible.

After two days, without any word from Lola or Gio, Charles called another meeting. We gathered in the hotel conference room to meet with Carlos and Efrain. It was time to decide what to do. The TSA's were finalized and ready to be presented to Tomas and his team, but we still had no word from Gio or Lola. There wasn't much consensus on what we should do. As we sat in the meeting I started to wonder if maybe I should go home. Maybe we should all go home? We didn't sign up to be working against the cartels. Maybe it was better if we all got out of harm's way.

"None of us like this," Carlos said. "But we are trying to find a way to resolve the situation. We want our Timbre employees to be able to transition to PacSouth, but we also need to get Lola back."

"We are going to make some concessions, yes," said Jake. "But we think in the end we're doing the right thing for everyone involved."

"So, let's go ahead and start with the TSAs that we know are not a concern," Charles said. "The ones where we don't think Tomas will push back on us. Perhaps if we present those to him and he's feeling favorable toward them he'll release Lola back to us. We all know finishing this deal is in his best interest."

"Great," said Jake. "Accounting seems to be the one that he was most sensitive to, so let's discuss payroll."

"The network towers TSA is definitely one we should save for last. That will be the most contentious." Ricardo chimed in.

I was typing notes on my laptop, but I was barely registering what I was typing. *What was the point anymore?* Every good feeling I'd had since I arrived in Mexico City had evaporated in the last week. Someone I thought I could trust turned out to be untrustworthy. Someone I thought was unbreakable, had been kidnapped. There was no way I belonged somewhere where that could happen. I was so lost in thought that I hardly realized Carlos and Jake had stopped talking abruptly.

I looked up and did a double take as I saw them walk into the room.

Lola looked tired and disheveled but unharmed. And Gio, with a black eye and a cut on his upper lip.

"Lola!" Ricardo jumped out of his seat and ran to embrace her. Chela followed suit.

"Are you okay? Ay que no! ¿Que pasa?" Chela's eyes had filled with tears. The three of them hugged. Chela was sobbing.

"I'm fine, I'm fine," Lola insisted. "It's okay."

George approached Lola. "Let me see you. Are you okay?" Lola nodded and George embraced her. "We were so worried about you!"

I could barely move. I was in such shock. For a moment I wondered if I was dreaming. Was this really happening? Were they just back safe? I looked to Charles. His chest was heaving. Lola approached him and they hugged tight. "It's okay, Charles," she said. "I'm alright."

Gio moved toward me, and I felt myself stand.

"Blake..." he said. For an instant I was so happy to see him safe that I almost forgot everything that had transpired between us. He moved to wrap his arms around me, and then in an instant it all came rushing back and I pushed him away.

"What the hell is wrong with you?!" I screamed. Every bit of emotion I hadn't let myself feel in days poured out of me. "Where have you been?!" I was choking back tears. I was furious. I was confused. He tried to close the space between us, but I pushed him away again. I raised my hand to slap his face when suddenly Max was between us, catching my arm.

"Whoa, Blake!" he said.

"I'm sorry!" Gio exclaimed. "I can explain!"

"Well, you better, man," Max interjected. "Because no one in this room trusts you at the moment."

"Screw you, Gio!" I spat out. Furious with him. Tears streaming down my cheeks.

"Please let me explain!" Gio begged.

"I can explain for him..."

I looked up and saw Sam had entered the room.

CHAPTER TWENTY-THREE
El Regreso

"What the hell is he doing here?" I spat out, angrily. "How could you?"

Ricardo began muttering obscenities under his breath and moved toward Sam with his fist raised.

"Hold on just a minute!" Gio shouted. "Sam isn't the enemy, here."

"Sam is the reason that I'm here!" Lola protested. "Just let them explain."

"Lola... ¿Es la verdad?" Chela asked.

"Sí," Lola replied.

"Everyone please sit down so we can find out what the hell is going on here!" Charles' voice cut through everyone else's. "Go ahead, Gio."

I turned and faced Gio, my anger still radiating out of me. *He better have a damn good explanation for what had happened.*

"Gracias," he said, sincerely. "I think we all knew that it was Tomas' people who had taken Lola. Obviously, we didn't know how serious the situation was at first, but it didn't seem like Tomas would want to have a murder overshadow his historic deal with PacSouth. Like I said before, I never knew him to be violent. I needed to talk to someone close to him, so I went to Sam. We grew up together and came up at Grupo Merced together and I knew he wasn't totally happy there." He turned to Sam. "¿Si claro?"

"Sí," Sam replied.

"So, we worked a few things out," Gio said. "And he took me to Lola."

"What does that mean?" I asked.

"Where did they take you, Lola?" Max asked.

"They took me to Tomas' fútbol stadium to try and scare me," Lola said. "I was restrained to a chair in the dark in the locker room." As she spoke, I noticed the bags under her eyes for the first time. Her hair was disheveled, and she had bruises on her wrist. I knew she was trying to be strong and minimize the experience, but underneath her tough exterior, I imagined she was pretty shaken up.

"Jesus," George muttered.

"So, what happens now?" Charles asked Gio. "I'm guessing there are some complications in play now that Lola is not where Tomas put her."

"Yes," Gio said gravely. "I have to go back to Grupo Merced. That's the deal we made with Tomas."

"What?!" My voice exploded out of me. "No! You absolutely can't do that. Gio, no."

"Blake...all that matters is the team is safe and that Lola is back," Gio said.

"We need you to be safe too!" I said, my voice cracking with emotion. I felt the sharp sting of tears forming behind my eyes. "They hurt you! Look at your face."

"Don't worry, Bella. Sam and I have a plan."

"A plan?" I stammered. "What kind of plan? How can you trust him? He's one of them!"

"We can't get into the specifics right now, Blake," Sam interjected. "Lo Siento. Tomas will be suspicious if we're gone too long."

"I don't want to hear a *word* out of your mouth!" I yelled at Sam.

"I'll explain more as soon as I can," Gio said to me. He turned to Charles. "In the meantime, close the deal as soon as you can. For everyone's sake."

"Okay," Charles said.

"Gio, we need to go now," Sam urged. I felt my temper flare again. They started out of the room and as they passed me, Gio caught my hand for a moment and squeezed it.

"I'll call you, Bella. Todo va a estar bien," he said tenderly. *Everything will be okay.* I felt so helpless I wanted to cry or scream or hit something, but instead I just watched them go.

After a moment I heard hushed voices and Jake, George, and Charles were convening at one end of the conference table. I looked to Lola, and she smiled faintly at me. I was so relieved to have her back, but now my worries had shifted to Gio. I could tell in her expression that she knew that.

"It'll be okay," she mouthed to me. I nodded, praying she was right.

Chela asked Lola in Spanish if she wanted her to take her to the doctor and Lola nodded in agreement.

"Alright everyone," Charles spoke to the group again. "Let's go ahead and call it for the day. Lola, at the moment we have Ricardo and Chela posted up in the hotel with us, would you like a room as well?"

"Chela is going to take me to my doctor," Lola said.

"After that why don't you come back here, and we'll put you up in a beautiful room where you can rest and feel safe." Charles said tenderly.

I watched as tears formed behind Lola's eyes. "Gracias Charles."

"I'll speak to the hotel. In the meantime, my U.S. people, I think this might be a good time to book travel home for a week. In fact, I'm not suggesting, I'm insisting. Just spend the week at home until we sort everything out with corporate and PacSouth. Book travel as soon as you can, for tomorrow if there are tickets available."

"Are we booking return flights?" Max asked.

"No, not right now. I will let you know once we know more," Charles said. "Plan on coming back but maybe take your belongings with you just in case."

Everyone looked exhausted. It seemed like the right time to go home.

I stood up from my chair and walked over to Lola. I hadn't hugged her since she returned. As we embraced, I felt myself relax slightly. Sam had delivered her safely back to us, maybe Gio could trust him after all. "I'm so glad you're okay," I said into her neck. My eyes filled with tears, and I held on to her.

She squeezed me tight. "Me too."

We all packed up our things from the conference room and headed back to our rooms.

As I walked to the elevator bank, I sent a text to my parents telling them I was going back to Dallas within the next day or for a short break. Their enthusiastic replies pinged through within moments and for some reason it made me want to cry.

Back in my room, I pulled out one of my suitcases from the closet and began packing. For a moment I thought about calling the butler service to help me, but I decided that was silly. I was perfectly capable and more than that, I just wanted to be alone.

I finished packing and then opened my phone and bought a plane ticket for the following morning. I'd be back in Dallas in twenty-four hours, just in time for dinner. Then I texted Gio and let him know I was heading home tomorrow and that I wasn't sure when or if I'd be back. As I sent the message, I felt my heart break. Everything had changed in the last few days, and nothing felt certain anymore. The idea that I was leaving Mexico City before we'd completed the merger felt like a failure. Realizing that I was probably in love with Gio, and I might never see him again was devastating. My emotions were all over the place and I ended up sitting in a chair staring out the window until the glow of the sunset was completely gone, and the city was bathed in darkness.

Eventually, I showered and got myself into bed. I couldn't stop the nervous thoughts that were swirling around in my head. *What if something happened to Gio? What if Sam was playing him? What if he got hurt?* It made me sick to my stomach to think about anything happening to him.

I sighed audibly and closed my eyes. *Relax, Blake. Try and get some sleep.* I thought I heard a faint tapping on the door and then I grew frustrated with myself that I was so lost in my thoughts of Gio that I was imagining he was right outside my door.

Knock, knock. I sat up in bed. That was definitely an actual sound coming from my door. In an instant I thought maybe it was Tomas or his cronies and my heart kicked into overdrive.

I grabbed my phone just in case and quietly got out of bed and tip-toed towards the door. My pulse was thumping in my ears as I leaned up and looked through the peephole.

Then my heart did a triple somersault as I saw Gio's face. It was actually him! Standing there, looking nervous and eager.

I wrenched the door open, and his face lit up as he laid eyes on me.

"Bella!" he exclaimed. He threw his arms around me and I leaned into his chest.

"What are you doing here?" I said as I ushered him inside.

I closed the door and he put his arms around me. "I couldn't let you leave without saying goodbye," he said. "You don't know how many lies I had to tell to get out of their office and come here."

"Gio..." I felt my heart fall. "I don't want you to go back to that life. I don't want you to be on Tomas' leash. He's a bad man, and you could get hurt."

"Don't worry, Bella," he said tenderly. "Sam and I will be fine. As I mentioned, we have a plan to get away from Grupo Merced and Tomas forever."

"Tell me what the plan is," I said. "Let me help you."

"It's dependent on a few things happening and I won't know for sure for a few days. But as soon as I do, I'll tell you everything."

"What if something goes wrong?" I asked. "I can't stand the idea of something happening to you."

"It won't," he said. "I promise. And as soon as I'm safe, you'll be the first to know."

CHAPTER TWENTY-FOUR
Llorando en Aviones

It surprised me more than it seemed to surprise my seatmate when I started to cry as the plane backed away from the gate from Mexico City headed for Dallas. He turned to me and looked sympathetic. "Tampoco no me gustan los aviones." *I don't like planes either.*

I didn't know what to say, and clearly, I couldn't explain what I was emotional about. So, I just wiped away my tears, smiled and said, "Gracias."

I was frustrated leaving Mexico City this way. We all knew that Charles having asked us to pack our things meant that we might not be able to return any time soon. There was unfinished business between our client and our team, and regardless of the events that occurred I hoped that Global Core would allow us to finish what we started.

I also couldn't fathom the possibility of my time in Mexico being over and most of that feeling was because I couldn't possibly fathom not being with Gio again. Then of course, there was always the natural possibility that I wouldn't be with Gio again, because there was no future with Gio, and that realization cut through me like a knife. He lived in Mexico, I lived in Texas. It wasn't that many miles away from each other, but we were worlds apart.

The truth washed over me as the plane lifted into the sky and headed back toward my home country. Nothing was in my control and the end result of all of this could be complete and total heartbreak. Something inside of me began to ache. The pain felt like it was radiating from my core and coming out of my eyes in the form of enormous and persistent tears.

I tried not to disturb my seatmate, so I just turned my head toward the window and cried silently for the duration of the flight. Somewhere over the Gulf of Mexico I felt my eyelids start to get heavy and I slept until the plane landed.

When we exited the plane, I felt numb. I walked out to the curb and called an Uber. Then I texted my parents to let them know that I had landed safely.

Watching the city go by as the Uber driver drove me back to my apartment, it was impossible not to compare the skyline of Dallas to that of Mexico City and it made my heart hurt even more. When I arrived back at my apartment, I unlocked the door, dropped my bags on the floor and went straight to my bed without even turning a light on. I had barely kicked off my shoes before I climbed under the covers and then I stayed in the dark until I fell asleep.

When I awoke the next day, there was a split second where I felt like the trip home had been a dream and I was still in my bed at the St. Regis. Then it registered that I was back home in Dallas, and I sighed. My sheets didn't smell like the hotel's bedding and the room had a sort of damp feeling to it. It was clear that no one had opened a window here for a while.

I reached for my phone to check my messages. There were a few from my parents making sure I'd gotten home alright and there was one from Mia reminding me that we were supposed to go barhop on McKinney tonight, but there was nothing from Gio. I replied to Mia and my parents, and then I got up and opened the windows. It was late spring and there was a pleasant breeze blowing in the trees outside. As I felt it hit my skin, I began to feel a bit calmer and more positive.

I got myself in a shower and it was a treat to realize that I could open my mouth in there without the fear that I'd wind up with Montezuma's revenge. I brushed my teeth freely after my shower and then I walked into the kitchen and made coffee with water filtered out of the tap.

"So weird," I marveled. I went to my bags that were still on the floor and I removed my laptop. Charles had told us to enjoy our time off and not to worry about work emails for a few days, but I still felt like I needed to check in and make sure everything was okay.

There were only a handful of emails in my inbox. One from Charles making sure that everyone was home safely. One from Lola letting us know that she too was vacationing away from Mexico City in an undisclosed location to get some space away from Tomas. Chela was visiting her parents and Ricardo had flown to Miami for his time away. I wrote a separate email to Jake asking if there was anything I needed to do today, and he replied right away telling me to go enjoy some time off and not to worry about the deal. He would reach out as soon as he had news.

I felt restless and useless without any work to do. It was going to take some getting used to not being with my team and not working on the deal. I thought about doing my laundry but everything in my suitcase was clean and pressed thanks to the butler service at the St. Regis. I thought about cleaning my apartment, but aside from a little bit of dust, it was perfectly clean. In the end, I decided to call my hair salon and see if they had any last-minute appointments and luck seemed to be with me.

"Blake! Oh my god! You're back!" Carlie the receptionist knew me well. "Yes, lady, Amanda has a cancellation at noon. It's a little bit last minute but can you come in then?"

"Yes!" I answered. "See you then."

It was my first haircut since I had left for Mexico City, and I had to admit it did feel like a way to delineate a new chapter in my life. Whether I wanted to admit it or not, being home for a bit was kind of a new beginning. Things were different in Dallas, and it would be different if I went back to Mexico.

"So, tell me all about this trip!" Amanda gushed as she massaged her fingers into my scalp.

"Well, it's not over yet," I said. "I'm just home for a couple weeks. But it's been really interesting and wild."

"I hear things are *crazy* down there!" she said. "Don't get yourself kidnapped by the Cartels!" She burst into laughter, clearly joking but I didn't dare correct her.

"Ha!" I did my best to feign laughter. "Oh well, it's all very safe and secure. We have a security detail who's always around." I felt bad lying but I wasn't ready to talk about what really happened and I didn't want to deter people from visiting Mexico.

"Wow," she marveled. "Look at you! How fancy!"

"Yeah, he's pretty great," I said, smiling to myself.

"Wait...he's *pretty great?* Okay, spill the tea."

"Well..." *What was it about hairstylists that made you want to confess your deepest darkest secrets? Was it the scissors that were positioned so close to your skull?* Before I knew it, I found myself telling her all about Gio.

"Do you have a photo?" she asked. "Is he cute?"

I pulled my phone out of my pocket and opened my photos to show her a selfie of the two of us together. "Girl!" she squealed! "He is *so* cute! Is this love!?"

"Oh, I dunno," I said, shrugging. "I mean I'm not staying there forever, and I doubt he has any plans to move to Dallas."

"You never know," she said. "My roommate's sister was traveling around South America by herself a few years ago and she met this guy from Dublin while she was at a hostel in Colombia, I think... and they had a blast together."

"Wow."

"And then they kept in touch, and they decided they should both meet up later in Peru, because Machu Pichu was on both of their itineraries around the same time. So, get this! For the next couple of weeks, he was in Argentina I think, and she was in Chile, and they kept in touch initially via email, just emailing constantly every night, G-chatting, eventually Skype calls, and then finally they met up in Peru, and I shit you not, they are married now and live in New York."

"Are you serious?" I asked. "That's so sweet!"

"It's possible! You just never know what could happen when you have a connection with someone. If it's meant to happen, it just does, girl."

I left the salon feeling lighter. The fact that Amanda had just chopped a few inches off my hair's length might have had something to do with it, but her story gave me solace. If something was meant to be, it'll be. I smiled as I walked back to my car and as I reached for my keys in my purse, I felt my phone vibrate. I picked it up to see that I had a text from Gio. I smiled a giddy smile to myself as I opened the phone to read the text.

"I need to talk to you," it said. "We might have a problem."

I froze in place and could feel my stomach doing flips. I needed Gio to be okay.

CHAPTER TWENTY-FIVE
Soledad

I didn't hesitate before I dialed Gio's number. My heart rate began to pick up as the phone rang.

"Hang on," he said as he answered.

"Oh...okay," I replied.

I heard some ambient street noises in the background for a few minutes. It sounded like he was outside. "I'm back," he said. "Bella, I need to tell you something, but you cannot say a word yet, just listen, just in case this line isn't secure. We cannot discuss anything specific right now, no specific names or events that have transpired, does that make sense?"

"Yes," I agreed. My heart was pounding in my chest. "Are you okay? Are you safe? Is your friend safe?"

"Yes," he replied. "We are safe."

"Okay, good."

"My friend has informed me that there is going to be an issue with part of the deal and you're the only person who I know I can warn without having to go into specifics."

"What is the issue? Or what kind of issue?"

"It has to do with land involved in one of your TSAs. The one involving the network towers. The towers are on land where some people we both know are growing certain *crops*. ¿Comprende? They will be very protective of this land, and they will not want any people outside of their sphere of influence going there. This is going to cause a problem. You need to talk to Charles and Jake right away. They will know what to do."

"Okay," I said.

"I miss you," he said.

"I miss you too," I said. I felt my voice catch in my throat as I said this. "I want to come back soon."

"I'm not sure if you should, but I also know I really want to see you."

"Jake said he'll let me know when they know."

"Okay, well when you know, tell Lola. She knows how to reach me. I may have to get rid of this phone. I'll explain more later."

"Okay. Please be safe."

"I will. But call Jake and Charles right away and let them know."

"I will." He ended the call.

I immediately called Jake and asked him to conference Charles in. I told them what Gio had told me, word for word.

"Jesus," Jake said. "So, we were right, Grupo Merced is just a front for their drug operations."

"Is there a way to resolve this issue?" Charles asked. "Can we still close the merger without this Network TSA causing issues?"

"I'm not sure," Jake admitted. "I'll need to speak to Carlos next week and we'll see if we can sketch out a plan."

"Alright," Charles said. "Blake, thank you for coming to us with this information. And we'll be sure to thank Gio the next time we see him."

When the call ended, I felt better. I knew now that Gio was safe. I had done something productive. I had helped our client and the team. It felt like I could relax... a little bit.

I spent the afternoon going through my closet and sorting out things I wanted to donate. I didn't really see the point in unpacking my suitcase. It felt better leaving it packed on the floor in case I needed to leave at a moment's notice and head back to Mexico City. As I was folding old clothes and placing them in garbage bags to take to the Goodwill, my phone rang, and it was my folks wanting to talk.

"How does it feel to be home?" my mom asked.

"Pretty good," I said.

"How was the flight?" my dad asked.

"Fine," I said. "Just took a nap."

Talking to my parents about my time in Mexico was strange. On the one hand, they were both still wary about my having gone there, but on the other hand, they were also wanting to hear every detail of what I'd experienced. It felt strange giving them the entire rundown on the last few months, while also being mindful to leave out the parts that might upset them or lead me down a conversation path that I didn't want to go on.

"Has your Spanish improved?" my mom asked. "Have you been speaking it much?"

"Oh yeah," I said. "I got to speak Spanish a ton. Most of the team from the U.S. doesn't speak Spanish, so it was helpful to have a few of us that do. Plus, most of our meetings are in Spanish, so you could say I'm fluent now."

"So, what will you do now that the project is over?" my mom asked.

"Oh, well it's not over entirely," I said. "We're working remotely for a little while to get some time at home and then we should be heading back to close the deal."

"What? Really? You're going back?" My mother sounded worried.

"Yeah. Mom, I told you about this in my last email."

"I thought the plan had changed and you were done," she said.

"Almost done," I said, trying to sound upbeat so they would let this go. "I'll be back for good before you know it."

"We just want you to be safe, honey," said my dad. "We worry about you."

"I know," I said. "But don't worry I'm being safe."

After the call ended, I felt my energy dip. It was that old feeling of having to defend something to someone who didn't seem to understand it. It made me miss being back in Polanco with my team who understood the vastness of what we were trying to accomplish. Shortly thereafter, I got myself ready and headed out to Katy Trail Ice House to meet Mia for our girls' night out.

It was the first time I'd been out in an American bar in months. I felt strange walking in and hearing the hum of people speaking English, and not Spanish. "Culture shock is very real," I said to myself.

The Rangers game was blaring out of the speakers, and everywhere I looked were young college students and people in their mid-twenties talking loudly to one another. I almost shook my head to try and clear my vision because the sight felt so different.

"Blake! Over here!" I heard Mia's voice calling to me over the crowd. She was seated at a table near one of the fire pits.

I walked over and gave her a big hug. "Hi!" I squealed. "Oh my god, it's so weird being back!"

"I bet!" she said, hugging me back. "Do you want me to attempt to speak to you in Spanish?"

I laughed. "No, that's okay!" we sat down at the table and a server appeared within moments.

"Hi y'all! What can I get for ya?" she asked.

"Hola. ¿Como estás?" I said, and then caught myself. "Oops! Sorry..."

"She just got back from Mexico City!" Mia explained to the server.

"Oh wow! That sounds like fun!" said the server.

We ordered glasses of sangria and cheese fries, and then we started to catch up. It was always easy with Mia. She made it feel like no time had passed, even if we hadn't seen each other in months.

"How are things going over there?" she asked. "Are you feeling more comfortable with the job now?"

"Yes," I said. "It was weird at first, feeling like the youngest and most inexperienced, but I've been feeling more and more like I'm really a part of the team." The server returned with our drinks and our fries. It had been a while since I'd had greasy American food and the smell was intoxicating.

"That's great! Well cheers!" We clinked our goblets and then we both reached for the fries.

"I'm really missing everyone actually," I admitted, mouth full. "I mean, obviously I'm stoked to be here with you! But they've become kind of like family and it's been odd being away."

"I get that," she said. "God, these cheese fries are so good."

"So good!"

"How are things going with Gio?" she asked as she licked two of her fingers clean. "Is that still happening?"

"I *think* it's still happening," I said. "We've just been so busy finalizing this merger." It was so tempting to tell her about all the drama that was happening behind the scenes, but I just didn't feel right about sharing any of that until it felt like it was all handled.

"Are you going to keep in touch with him when you come home?" she asked.

"I hope so! I mean, we haven't really talked about it. There's just been so much stuff going on work-wise."

"You need to talk to him about it!" she said. "He seems really great! I think you should totally stay in touch with him!"

"I want to."

"It'll all work out Blake. Just don't stress and go with the flow."

"Ugh. You know that is hard for me."

"I know. It's probably good to have some time apart and clear your head."

"I guess."

"You know the saying absence makes the heart grow fonder. Maybe you'll both realize how you really feel about each other."

"I do really miss him," I admitted.

"Es la *passión!*" she joked.

Lying in my bed that night, all I could think about was Gio. Was Amanda right that when you had a connection with someone things just kind of worked out? Was Mia right that I needed to talk to him? I knew I should, but I wanted to wait until I saw him again. And the more that I thought about having that conversation the less I wanted to have it. There was a part of me that just wanted to spend unlimited time with Gio, exploring the city and each other without any distractions. Then there was also the part of me that was eager to get back to work with the team and end this game with Tomas and Sam once and for all.

Against my better judgement I decided to text him, "Hi. I miss you. Just lying in bed thinking about you wishing you were next to me." I waited a few minutes staring at my phone hoping he would text me back, but then my eyes grew heavy, and sleep pulled me under.

Monday morning came and I jumped out of bed and grabbed my laptop. I was praying to have an email in my inbox that would tell me it was time to come back to Mexico City and continue our work, but there wasn't anything like that. Jake had emailed to let me know that he had spoken with Carlos, and that they were attempting to figure out the Network TSA issue, but there wasn't really much work for me to do, other than to review the pending documents we had been preparing prior to Lola's disappearance.

I noticed that the language had been significantly softened, and the requests on behalf of Timbre and PacSouth had been paired down. It frustrated me that we were caving in in this way, but I knew it was Carlos and Jake's efforts to keep our team safe until the merger was behind us.

The time home felt like a total slog. I was in limbo waiting for good news or bad news, but there was simply no news. After three days, I started to villainize my apartment. Things that had never bothered me before suddenly drove me nuts. My washer and dryer didn't get the wrinkles out of my clothes the same way the butler service at the St. Regis did. My coffee wasn't as good as the coffee in Polanco. My sheets felt itchy. I dreamed of being back in my hotel room bed at the St. Regis, curled up in Gio's arms.

There was also fair amount of feeling sorry for myself. I tried to get out of the house as much as I could. I went for runs and walks on the Katy Trail. I tried ordering food from my favorite places, telling myself I wouldn't be eating at them for a while, but it did little to lift my spirits.

Finally, at the end of the week I got an email from Jake asking if it was a good time to call. I told him it was, and I practically jumped when my cell phone began to ring.

"Jake! Hi!" I exclaimed. "What's up?" It was hard to mask my enthusiasm.

"Hey Blake, so we have some news."

"Okay..."

"Given the importance of the PacSouth relationship in the U.S., we are going to be heading back to Mexico City on Monday. Corporate has given us the go ahead to try and wrap up the deal with Grupo Merced, and Carlos and I are working on the Network TSA situation."

"Great!" I exclaimed. There was silence on the other end. "Is there something else?"

"Yeah," Jake said. "George has decided not to join us for the rest of this deal. He and his wife aren't comfortable with what's gone on and he's going to go ahead and finish the rest of the deal remotely and then take a little time off."

"Oh, wow." I felt my heart sink. George and I had become close since we'd been abroad, and I was truly going to miss him. "I'll give him a call."

"I'm sure he'd appreciate that," Jake said. "How are you feeling about coming back? It would be more than understandable if you wanted to stay home."

"No, I want to come back," I said earnestly. "I want to finish what we started."

"Okay," he said. "If you're sure, go ahead and book travel for Monday and let me know when you're back at the St. Regis."

No sooner had Jake ended the call that I dialed George's cell. He answered on the third ring. "So, I guess you heard, huh?"

"I did," I said. "We're really going to miss you."

"I will miss you guys too, but the Disney Cruise line is calling, and I know it'll put Sheryl at ease to know that I'm safe."

We chatted for a few minutes, reminiscing about our favorite memories of our time in Mexico City. It was bittersweet, reliving the good times but knowing that when we returned, we'd be without George.

"I really hope you enjoy your trip," I said. "And I hope we get to work together again soon."

"I hope so too," he said. "Keep your head up, Blake... and please be careful."

"I will."

CHAPTER TWENTY-SIX
El Corazón

Sitting on the plane heading back to Mexico City I was feeling every emotion. I was nervous, I was excited. I wanted to get there as quickly as possible to see Gio and the rest of my team, but I was also worried if we were really safe going back to the office.

The flight was bumpy going over the Gulf of Mexico, but I hardly noticed because I was so in my head. As soon as Jake had told me I had the greenlight to fly back, I texted Gio and let him know.

"Send me your flight number and I'll pick you up," his reply had read.

When the plane landed, most of my anxieties faded away and all I could think about was him. My lips curled into the giddiest grin because I knew it was only a matter of minutes before I saw him again. I'd always been a patient flyer; the kind of person who remains seated even after the fasten seatbelt sign went off. I'd simply never seen the point in standing up when you know that a dozen other passengers have to deplane before you can even make your way into the aisle. But today, I was on my feet before the captain even had time to say, "Bienvenidos a la Ciudad de Mexico." If there hadn't been other passengers, I would have run off the plane, and down the jetway as fast as my feet would carry me to where he'd be meeting me at baggage claim.

Instead, I waited my turn to deplane, my foot tapping impatiently against the carpeted floor of the aircraft. I kept pace with the other passengers as we climbed up the jetway as not to seem too eager, but when I was finally inside the airport, I picked up pace.

Going through immigration felt like an eternity. I couldn't stop checking the time. When they finally stamped my passport, I felt myself sigh with relief.

Right on cue, my heart started to kick into overdrive as I boarded the escalator descending towards the airport exit. My eyes started searching for him in the crowd of people. My stomach turned with excited nerves, and I could feel my palms beginning to sweat. As I stepped off the escalator, I continued to search for him in the sea of other passengers and their loved ones, but I couldn't spot him. There was something exciting and romantic about people reuniting at airports. Getting to share moments with people they hadn't seen in a while. It always warmed my heart.

Finally, I spotted him, leaning against a column near the exit. He looked unbelievably cool in a T-shirt and jeans, wearing the cowboy hat I had bought for him. In his hands he held a sign that said, "Bienvenidos, Bella Blake" on it.

The second our eyes met his face exploded into an excited smile. We moved toward each other as fast as we possibly could, while navigating the crowd, but it felt like slow motion. When my body finally crashed into his, he threw his arms around me and lifted me off the ground. Without thinking, I wrapped my legs around his waist, and we kissed. I heard several people around us laugh, or sigh. There were a few, "awww's" and some clapping but I didn't care. I didn't care what was going on around us because I was back in Gio's arms, and it felt more like home than any person or place I'd encountered during my time in Dallas.

He carried my bags and we walked to his truck. He opened my door for me and then climbed in himself.

"I want to take you to dinner tonight," he said. "But I'm supposed to be playing for the other team now, so I was thinking maybe we could eat in your hotel room?"

Twist my arm. "Okay. That works."

"Manuel will be escorting you all to the office from now on but know that I'll be keeping an eye on things at Grupo Merced and Sam, and I have a direct line of communication with Carlos now." He reached into his pocket and showed me a second phone.

We drove out of the parking structure, out of the airport and onto the road toward the city center. "So, I'm still not clear on what the plan is," I said. "What are you going to do?"

"We are planning to leave."

"Good. You should just work for Global Core and tell Tomas it's over."

"No, Blake...We're going to leave Mexico City...in fact we're going to leave Mexico all together."

"What?" I was stunned. "Leave Mexico? But you love Mexico! It's your home!"

"I know, Bella." He sounded sad. "But if I stay, and if Sam stays, we will always be in danger. Not just from Tomas, but from his family and the men who work for them."

"Where are you going to go?"

"We're not sure yet," he admitted. "Sam has some contacts in Guatemala, and also Costa Rica. We're trying to figure out the safest place for us to go where these men cannot follow."

"Become a little surf bum in Costa Rica?" I laughed trying to lighten the mood.

In that instant I almost wanted to ask him about us, but I was still nervous about what that conversation might mean and for now I just wanted to enjoy him.

As we drove into the city, I felt my heart lift seeing the skyline again. The buildings, the cars, the traffic, the busses, the people. It felt good to be back. I knew things were going to be chaotic with the remainder of the merger, and of course I had no idea what was going to happen with Gio, but at least this was a familiar chaos that I'd become accustomed to since the beginning of the year and a chaos I choose for myself.

It was evening as we arrived back at the St. Regis, but the sky was glowing, and it felt like the sun would hover indefinitely at the horizon for hours and hours.

We spent the evening curled up in my bed eating takeout and drinking Pacificos in our robes. I loved talking with Gio. I never laughed as hard as I did when I was with him and watching him laughing with me filled me with joy. He was so serious in his everyday life that when I caught him in moments of fun and silliness it thrilled me. I told him all about my time in Dallas, how much I'd missed Mexico City and how two places can feel so much like home.

"I think I finally understand 'home is where the heart is,'" I joked.

"You're adorable." He smiled at me.

"It's weird to think that we're all still kind of in danger," I said. "I mean something bad could happen at any moment. But I don't worry about that when I'm with you."

He chuckled. "It's a strange place to be, isn't it? Finding joy in the midst of all of this."

"Yes. Exactly."

He stacked our food containers and moved them outside the room. "I think things will all work out."

My stomach tightened. He'd just given me a perfect segue to talk about us and all of a sudden, I was terrified to say anything. I watched him fiddle with items on the bar and finally he grab us each a bottle of water. As he walked back to the bed, he smiled at me, and his eyes seemed to twinkle. He settled back into the bed next to me and my heart began to ache. I didn't want this to end. I just wanted to stay in this blissful denial and forget that my days with Gio were numbered.

He must have noticed my mood shift because he reached over and touched my face to redirect my gaze back towards his eyes. "Are you okay?" he asked.

"Yeah, sorry," I said.

"What are you thinking about?" he asked. I shook my head and just leaned into his chest, and he seemed to understand. "You are thinking about us, aren't you?"

"Yeah," I admitted shyly. "I don't want it to end."

"I don't want it to end either," he said. "I care for you very much."

"I feel the same way," I admitted. "Will we ever see each other again?"

"I hope so," he said. "You never know where life can lead."

"That's what I hear."

"But if this is the only time we'll have had together, then I have nothing but gratitude because it was amazing." He leaned down and kissed the top of my head. "And if life brings us back to each other again later, what a perfect surprise that would be."

"Very true," I said. He reclined his posture and leaned against the pillows, and I nestled against his chest. He ran his fingers through my hair and held me tightly to him.

"Blake?" he whispered.

"¿Si?"

"Te quiero mi amor."

"I love you too, Gio." I looked up into his sweet eyes and then he kissed me. It was a kiss that was full of everything we had experienced, and everything we couldn't find words to articulate. It was happy, sad, sweet, and bitter all at the same time. After a while, I rested my head against his chest and eventually drifted off to the sound of his steady heartbeat.

When I woke up in the morning, Gio was gone, but on the pillow next to me was the cowboy hat and a note folded on the brim. I opened it and it read, "This hat always seemed to fit you better than me. I hope when you wear it, and it reminds you of our time together and makes you smile. Te amo."

CHAPTER TWENTY-SEVEN
Tensión

Going back to work Monday morning felt like going back to school after winter break. I was excited to be there, but also realizing that the downtime was over, and it was time to get back to work was a bit of an adjustment. Manuel was in the lobby to escort Charles, Jake, Max, and I to the office. It was different without George there, and I felt his absence. I missed his sense of humor and his brotherly quarrels with Jake, but I kept thinking of him in the middle of the Caribbean with his family on a Disney cruise and that made me smile.

When we arrived at the office, Lola, Chela, and Ricardo were all there. Their early arrival made it clear that we needed to focus to get the deal done. There wouldn't be any long lunches this week, that was for sure. Carlos was also there. He was planning to be in the rest of our meetings until the merger was done. It seemed that he wanted to both oversee the rest of the negotiations and be there to help if need be. He had a unique way of handling Tomas, which I suspected is why he had risen in the ranks at PacSouth so quickly.

"Alright, team welcome back," Charles said as we all sat down in the conference room. "As you know, tomorrow we will be meeting with Grupo Merced for what will hopefully be one of our last meetings."

I looked at Lola, worried that she'd be triggered, but she looked stoic.

"I will be there tomorrow to help with the negotiations," Carlos said. "I know that Tomas and his guys are tough, and we want to make sure that we can get this last piece handled so that we can all move on. I want to thank you all for returning to complete this project. I know it's been a stressful one."

"You can say that again," Max said. There was a bit of stifled laughter around the table.

"So here are the TSA's we'll be hoping to close out tomorrow," Jake said. "Accounting, facilities, legal, payroll, benefits, HR operations, data management, data migration and the one we know is going to cause a little bit of tension, the network TSA which includes the maintenance of network towers."

"Correct," Charles said. "We know that the biggest point of contention is going to be the network towers that are on Grupo Merced's land."

"Also known as cartel land," Ricardo said.

"That is what we're going to assume," Carlos said. "Yes."

"Tomas is never going to go for that," Lola said. "If PacSouth has access to those towers, that means they will have access to where Grupo Merced is growing their mota."

"Their what?" Max asked.

"Marijuana," Lola answered. "And who knows what else."

"Probably coca leaves..." Ricardo said. "Or poppies."

"Okay, well we don't know every reason why they might be protective of the land, but we can assume based on the information we received from Gio and Sam that it's property they won't want to share."

"So, what do we do?" I asked.

"We're honestly not sure," said Charles. "We're going to start by asking for access to the land with Grupo Merced's permission to inspect the towers, and from there we will try to negotiate supervised visitations to the land to service the towers going forward."

"It's the best idea we have at the moment," Jake said. "PacSouth needs access to the towers to ensure the success of their investment. Anything we can do to make sure we secure that is key."

I looked to Lola again and she was shaking her head. She seemed to think it wouldn't work.

"What happens if we can't come to an agreement on the network TSA?" Chela asked.

Jake, Charles, and Carlos all looked at each other as if they didn't want to jinx anything by answering her question.

"The merger could collapse," Lola answered. "And hundreds of people could potentially lose their jobs. Right?"

No one said anything for a moment. Then Carlos spoke. "It's far more likely that we will come to some kind of agreement."

"We are going to do everything in our power to make sure that doesn't happen," Charles said. "For the rest of the day, please spend your time going over everything we're presenting tomorrow. Triple check that every 'i' is dotted and every 't' is crossed. I don't want Tomas to be able to question any of our work. Let's get going team."

The rest of the day was a blur. I spent the day re-reading the same documents I'd been reading for months and occasionally, my eyes would begin to glaze over, and I'd go to the vending machine to get myself a drink and some M&Ms.

It was hard not having Gio in the office with us. There were so many moments over the last few months when having mid-day coffee breaks with him kept my spirits up. Occasionally I'd look over to the chair where he always sat reading his books, expecting to see him there, but instead it was just Manuel staring straight ahead, taking his job very seriously.

At the end of the day, we were escorted back to the hotel by Manuel. I went to my room and climbed into bed. I was exhausted and nervous about what we hoped was the final meeting tomorrow. I had been so wrapped up in my excitement to see Gio again that I'd nearly forgotten I'd have to be in the same room as Tomas again, after we all knew what he'd done to Lola.

I had a hard time sleeping that night. I tossed and turned, having dreams about kidnappings, looming network towers, and fields of coca leaves blowing in the wind. At one point in the night, I reached my hand over for Gio hoping he was there with me somehow. When I woke up in the morning, I had a looming sense of dread that something bad was going to happen.

Arriving at the Grupo Merced offices was tense. I wanted to be stoic and calm like Lola, but I found my hands were shaking slightly as I reached into my bag for a pen and paper to take notes.

"You okay?" Max asked me quietly.

I nodded at him. "Yeah."

"It'll be okay," he assured me. "We got this."

I wish I shared his confidence. I looked around the table at my team, my family, I felt such a fierce sense of love and protection for all of them. I wanted to reach out and hug them all. I prayed silently that things would be okay and that all would go well.

Carlos and Efrain came into the meeting next and seated themselves at the table. Carlos gave us all an assured nod. I gripped my hands against my pant leg, willing them to stop shaking.

Eventually, Tomas entered the meeting, followed by Sam, then Gio and the rest of his team. I winced seeing Gio with them, pretending to be one of them. I hoped he'd catch my eye, but he ignored me. As they sat down, I felt Tomas' eyes on me, so just as we had planned, I glared at Gio, feigning feelings of intense betrayal. Out of the corner of my eye I saw Tomas smile and I decided he must have been satisfied with my performance.

Carlos rose from his seat to welcome everyone and thanked them for attending the meeting today. "I know we're all eager to wrap things up and move on," he said. "So, thank you to everyone who has come out today."

Tomas nodded. "Let's just get it done," he said.

The plan was for Carlos to begin with the Network TSA. We knew that it would be the most difficult discussion, so we figured we'd rather not save it until later in case it blew up the rest of the deal. We figured present him with the bad news first, so that everything else was smooth sailing.

"Right," Carlos said. "So, we've decided to start with the TSA agreement that we have the most questions about. And that is the Network TSA."

"Alright," Tomas said.

"The Timbre team is requesting access to the network towers in order to service and ensure the towers are appropriately maintained."

"No," Tomas began. We had been expecting this, but it still caught me by surprise and my blood pressure began to rise. *Why did this man have to be such a nightmare?* "That land belongs to Grupo Merced."

"Right," Carlos treaded lightly. "But the towers belong to Timbre and are critical to the long-term success of Timbre at PacificSouth."

"Timbre will still be able to use the towers for their network, but they will not have access to the land," Tomas said coolly. "There is no need to have access to them. They are in perfect working order."

"Tomas, with all due respect, the network towers are the most important part of the sale for PacSouth. How much would it cost to buy the land so that the towers can be operated and maintained by us?"

"The land is not for sale," Tomas said.

I felt my legs shaking even more. I turned to Lola, but I couldn't read her expression. I was starting to wonder if what she had said might happen. *Would the sale collapse right here and now?*

"What if we establish a TSA in perpetuity," Charles suggested. "Say that Grupo Merced will forever service the network towers as long as the PacSouth owns Timbre."

"For free," Carlos added. "And PacSouth will still want access to them once a year to make sure that they are up to our standards, under the supervision of Grupo Merced, of course."

This was it. This was the 'Hail Mary' that Carlos, Jake and Charles were throwing in hopes that Tomas would accept, and we could proceed. Aside from this strategy they didn't have another plan. This was the make-or-break moment.

Tomas didn't say anything. He just stroked his chin in thought. He looked like an actual plotting villain, and I narrowed my eyebrows in anger. "Alright," he said. "PacificSouth will have to pay for any service updates on the towers, but we will maintain them monthly for free."

I felt a collective exhale in the room as everyone's relief washed over them. I almost had the impulse to smile, but there was something in my gut that wasn't letting me get too excited yet.

"Thank you, Tomas," Carlos said. "I'd like to send one of our guys over to review the state of the towers this week."

"Alright," Tomas said. "They can have one hour."

Carlos leaned over to Efrain and whispered something in his ear. Efrain nodded. "Okay," Carlos said. "Efrain will go tomorrow."

"As you wish," Tomas said.

Over the course of the next hour, we outlined the rest of the TSA's for Tomas. He seemed to be uncharacteristically understanding about everything and I didn't trust how calm he was. *Was something going on behind the scenes?* I looked to Gio trying to read his expression, but he was totally deadpan. *I bet he's great at poker*, I thought.

"Okay, we will work to get the final documents drawn up this week for signature now that all TSAs have been agreed upon," Jake said. "Thank you everyone for the support."

"Alright," Tomas grumbled and then got up from his seat. Jake reached across the table to shake his hand, but Tomas simply nodded and walked out the door, with Gio, Sam and the rest of his team in hot pursuit. Carlos, Efrain, and Charles moved to the side of the room to talk.

"That was surprisingly easy," Max said to me.

"We still need to see if Tomas signs and keeps up his end of the bargain," Ricardo said.

"Right," I said. "I don't like how calm he was. It was unnerving."

"Agreed," Lola chimed in. "Tomas cannot be trusted. We need to be on high alert."

Carlos walked over to where our little group was standing. "Great job everyone! This is a success! PacSouth will be very happy!" He and Efrain left the room looking victorious. I wanted to share in their celebration, but my uneasy stomach wouldn't allow it.

CHAPTER TWENTY-EIGHT
Sorpresas

The next night, we all sat around the table at Ponte Vecchio, which was Charles' favorite Italian restaurant in Polanco. He had ordered a couple celebratory bottles of Brunello for the table and after filling everyone's glasses, he raised a toast.

"Well, team we did it!" he said. "The paperwork has been sent over to legal! Congratulations everyone, you did a spectacular job!"

We raised our glasses.

"How did the inspection go at the towers?" Lola asked.

"I spoke with Carlos on the way here," Jake said. "He's waiting to get the report back from Efrain and he'll let us know as soon as he does."

Despite my earlier concerns, it appeared that things had indeed gone as planned, while we were waiting for our dinner, I excused myself to the ladies' room and tried to call Gio. The call went straight to voicemail, so I left a message.

"Hi," I said "So it looks like everything has been sent over to legal and we're nearly done here. I'll be booking travel soon and heading home next week. I want to see you before I go. Let me know when you can sneak away." I paused before hanging up. "Te quiero!" I couldn't help but smile as I said it.

I returned to the table just as the servers were bringing out plates of pasta and a wheel of parmesan cheese. Each person's pasta was placed into the wheel of cheese and stirred until it was coated in the desired amount.

The meal was exquisite, and a hush fell over the table as everyone hungrily dug into their pasta. It was uncharacteristically quiet at our normally chatty table, aside from the occasional moan of yummy delight, so I decided it was as good a time as any to thank the team for making me feel so welcomed. I lightly tapped my fork on my wine glass, and everyone looked up.

"I just wanted to say thank you to all of you for this experience," I began. "I wasn't sure what to expect. And I am so thankful for how patient you all were with me and for showing me the ropes. And especially to Charles and Jake who took a chance on someone as inexperienced as I was. Thanks for having faith in me."

"We're glad to have you here with us," Charles said.

"Keep pushing, chica!" said Lola. "You're going to go far at Global Core."

"Here, here!" said Max. And everyone raised their glasses.

I felt my eyes well up with tears and I blinked them away with a smile.

The next morning started like any other. I got ready, got myself downstairs to the lobby, met the rest of the team and Manuel drove us to the office. I had the strangest feeling like I'd forgotten something, but I looked in my bag and I had everything I needed.

"Blake, you awake?" Max teased me in the car.

"Yeah," I said. "I don't know why I feel like I forgot something."

"Do you have your phone?" he asked.

I reached into my bag and pulled it out. I glanced down at the screen but still no texts or calls from Gio.

When we arrived at the office, Chela was already there, working quietly. Ricardo arrived shortly thereafter and got to work on his laptop. We had scheduled a meeting with Carlos and Efrain this morning to discuss the status of the network towers and it was nice to know we were all in the office and ready to go on time.

Manuel offered to go on a food run for breakfast tacos, Jake and Charles were chatting off to the side discussing the finalization of the deal and the follow up work to come, and Max was in the kitchen helping himself to coffee. I got up to get myself some coffee, and as I walked out into the hallway, I saw the receptionist there, filing her nails. She smiled at me as I passed.

I walked into the kitchenette and made myself a cup of coffee. I added cream and sugar and grabbed a breakfast pastry as well. Then I headed back toward the conference room.

"Hola," I heard a voice say. "Tengo un paquete para Global Core." I looked up to see a young delivery man holding a box with an office supply logo on the side. He looked nervous.

"Tomaré eso." The receptionist let him know she could take the package. He set it on the floor. It looked heavy.

I wasn't sure why, but I stood there rooted to the spot watching. The next few moments happened in what felt like slow motion. The delivery man hurried out of the building, the receptionist pulled out a pair of scissors and cut open the box. I watched as she opened the cardboard flaps and then saw her grab her own mouth and vomit onto the floor next to her. Then she hit her knees and fainted, her head hitting the floor with a sickening thud.

"Holy shit," I cried. "Someone, get help!" I ran over to her to check and make sure she was okay, but as I dropped to my knees to help her, I saw out of the corner of my eye, a red viscous liquid oozing out of the bottom corners of the box.

"Jake! We need help!" I screamed. Jake ran over, followed by Ricardo, Chela, Max, and Charles. Jake observed the scene and then peered into the box and that was when I heard him say it.

"Madre de dios, es una cabeza."

For an instant I felt like I was also going to throw up, but then I felt like I was having an out of body experience. Some kind of calm came over me, maybe it was the gut feeling I'd had that something bad was going to happen or maybe it was the adrenaline.

"What did he just say?" Charles asked. "Did he say a head?!"

I heard Jake say it again, "Es una cabeza..."

"Yes," I answered Charles.

"Oh, hell no," I watched Max run toward the bathroom and then I heard him retching.

I looked at Jake. "¿Que piensas? Who do you think it is?"

"I'm not sure." His voice was quivering.

I looked to Charles. He just stood there stunned, Chela was crying, Ricardo's hands were in his hair. The receptionist was still out cold.

"Jake, call security," I heard my voice say.

"Huh?" He was in shock.

"Call security!" I yelled. "Everyone into the conference room now."

Security rushed into the office and outside I heard the sirens as an ambulance pulled up to the building. "Gio, where are you?" I screamed into my phone. "Call me! Please!"

"Where is Lola?" Ricardo yelled, sounding horrified. He picked up his phone and jammed it to his ear.

Then Charles' cell phone exploded with rings. He answered it. "Carlos? Where are you? Are you safe? No, he's not here."

"Who?" Jake demanded.

"Hold on," Charles said. He covered the bottom of his phone. "Carlos doesn't know where Efrain is."

In that instant, Lola rushed into the office and then stopped square in her tracks as she saw the scene. "What is going on?" she demanded. She rushed into the conference room. "Is everyone okay? Why are there police and paramedics here!?"

"Someone mailed a head to the office." Max was lying with his head on the table, scared to move for fear that he'd pass out.

"Where is Gio?" Lola demanded. "Blake, is he okay?!"

"I..." My voice failed.

"Mija!" she ran over to me and put her arms around me.

"I can't get a hold of him." I felt myself break in her embrace and I began to sob uncontrollably.

Charles was still on the phone with a panicked Carlos, telling him not to come here and to get somewhere safe immediately.

"Carlos doesn't know where Efrain is," Jake told Lola.

I continued to cry in her arms. Manuel burst into the room. "We are clearing the area now! Everyone is going back to the hotel! Get your things."

We were rushed out of the office by Manuel and the security team and shuttled back to the hotel. I kept dialing Gio's number, but it continued to go straight to voicemail.

Once back at the St. Regis we were all hustled into the conference room while Charles received instructions from corporate and Manuel and Rafael swept our hotel rooms.

We sat there as corporate spoke to all of us over the speakerphone. We were to pack our things immediately and they were booking tickets for us to leave Mexico City before the end of the day. Lola, Ricardo, and Chela would have security for a few weeks until they could confirm they were safe.

I felt like I was in a bad dream just watching everything happen around me. Time was nonsense. The call from the corporate office could have lasted an hour, or it could have been five minutes. I had no idea.

Eventually we got the greenlight from Rafael and Manuel to return to our rooms. We had half an hour to pack and be ready to leave for the airport. We were not to open our doors for anyone until either Rafael or Manuel returned to collect us. No butlers, no room service. Nothing.

I walked into my room and looked around. All I wanted was to curl up in the bed and disappear, but instead I needed to rush to get everything packed.

I didn't bother to fold anything, I just jammed all of my things into my suitcases. I checked all of the wall sockets for chargers, I double checked under the bed. I checked all the drawers and cabinets in the bathroom. I finally got everything into my suitcase, changed my clothes and heard a knock at the door just as I was zipping the last bag closed.

"Señorita Blake, es Manuel!" I heard at the door.

"I'm coming!" I called.

I checked the peep hole and then opened the door for Manuel. He and the butler gathered my bags and then ushered me downstairs. As we walked down to the lobby, I saw Lola, Chela, and Ricardo standing there with another security guard I didn't recognize. I broke away from Manuel and the butler and ran to hug them. My eyes filled with tears. They all looked scared.

"Please, be safe," I said through my tears. "Please email and let us know that you are okay."

"We will," Ricardo said. His eyes were red.

"Señorita Blake, we must go," Manuel said. I took one last look at Chela, Ricardo, and Lola and then ran after Manuel and the butler toward the car.

Charles, Max, and Jake were already inside with their luggage. Manuel got in the driver seat and before I even had a moment to look back at the St. Regis we were peeling out of the driveway and onto the road.

Charles was on the phone with corporate assuring them that we were headed to the airport.

"Still nothing from Efrain," Jake said. I didn't know how to feel. "And they still haven't identified the...the person..."

I was terrified to hope. I could never wish any harm on someone as kind as Efrain, but I needed Gio to be alive.

We arrived at the airport, and I barely registered we had checked in for our flights. I walked with Jake, Max, and Charles to the departure area, and we sat at a table at the Starbucks. They were all leaving more than an hour before me, but it was nice to sit with them until they had to go. No one said much. We were all in a state of shock.

"Well, I'm glad the team is safe," Max said, breaking the silence.

"Me too," Jake said.

"Agreed," Charles said looking up from his coffee

"Blake, I'm sure Gio is okay," Jake said, his voice cracking slightly. "He has to be."

I couldn't speak. I just nodded my head. I sipped my tea until one by one it was time for them all to go. "Everyone text when you land, okay?" Charles insisted as he departed first. We all agreed, and we hugged each other and said our goodbyes. Jake was the next to leave and then finally Max's flight announced they were boarding.

"Are you going to be okay flying back alone?" Max asked. I nodded "Let's try not to panic until we know something for sure. Gio is smart. I am sure he's alright."

Max gave me a big hug and then he walked away

I decided to text Mia, "Something terrible happened. I'll explain later. I'm coming home."

Immediately my phone rang, it was Mia, "Are you okay?"

"I'm safe, but I'm not okay," I burst into tears.

"Blake... What is it?"

"I don't know where Gio is."

"What time do you land? I'll pick you up."

"I think seven o'clock," I sobbed.

"It'll be okay! I'll be there."

I boarded my flight and found my seat. The plane was half empty and I was grateful. As the safety demonstration began, it became clear that I would have the row to myself, so I shifted into the middle seat, fastened the seatbelt, and then laid down. I buried my face in my sweatshirt and I sobbed.

I cried as the plane taxied and left the gate. I cried as the plane hurdled down the runway. I cried even harder as we ascended into the sky, and I continued to cry as we leveled out. After about an hour, I felt my eyes begin to get heavy and I closed them. Breathing deep, I tried to calm myself down and remind myself that I needed to handle things one moment at a time. For that moment, I was in flight and there was nothing more to do than lie there and breathe.

The plane landed with a thud, and I was jerked awake. Somewhere over the gulf, I had once again cried myself to sleep. My body felt like a pile of sandbags. I didn't want to move. I just wanted to disappear.

As the plane taxied to the gate, I reached for my phone and turned it on. As I got service, a slew of text messages popped up on my phone. The first was from Jake to the group, saying that he'd landed safely in Miami. Then one from Max that he'd landed safely in L.A., then there was one from Charles to our group. He was on a layover in Philly but wanted us to know that Carlos had informed him that they had identified Efrain as the victim of the murder.

"Oh my god!" I gasped. I could feel the tears of relief rolling down my face.

I felt terrible for Efrain's friends and family. He was a caring, smart, man and I knew Chela, Ricardo and Lola would grieve this loss. But I was so relieved that it wasn't Gio. I felt like for the first time in hours I could actually breathe.

Jake had asked on the thread if we knew what was going to happen with the deal? And did they know anything about what had happened to Efrain.

Charles said they were still waiting on information, and he'd let us know as soon as he heard anything, but Carlos had heard that Tomas' brother Mateo had gotten involved after our last meeting, and he feared that Mateo might be to blame for Efrain's murder. As for the status of the merger, PacSouth would be making that decision on their own as Global Core had pulled our support from the deal.

As I moved to gather my belongings, I noticed my hands were shaking. Images of the bloody box kept flashing into my head. I squeezed my eyes tight trying to will them away.

I felt numb walking off the plane, through customs and down to baggage claim. When I arrived at the baggage carousel, there was Mia, standing, waiting for me. Without thinking I walked straight to her and fell into her arms. I sobbed harder than I had ever sobbed before. It was like the entirety of the last few months just came pouring out of me and she was on the receiving end of every emotion I had felt. She held on to me tight and stroked my hair.

"It's okay," she said. "I'm here."

When we got back to the house, Mia made a call to order us dinner and she opened a bottle of wine.

I sat on the couch with her and told her everything top to bottom. Every single detail since I had left on this assignment. All the drama with Sam and Lola, and every detail of Gio... about Tomas and how his brother might now be involved. Efrain's murder... How I had no idea if Carlos, Chela, Lola or Ricardo would remain safe. Or if the violence would continue. How I didn't know where Gio was, if he was safe, or if I'd ever see him again. There was so much to process.

Mia sat and listened to every word. She handed me tissues while I cried, she made me a plate when the food arrived and refilled my wine glass. And at the end of the night, she stayed until I fell asleep on the couch, and she covered me in a blanket.

When I woke up in the morning, I checked my phone. Still nothing from Gio. My heart wrenched with worry. I got up and got into my bed and then I slept until almost noon.

I checked my phone again and this time I did have text message notifications.

Charles had chimed back in on the group thread. According to Carlos, The Mexican police had just arrested Tomas Barajas and he had implicated his brother Mateo Barajas in the murder of Efrain Solis. They didn't know what was going to happen with the merger, but it appeared for the time being that justice might be served.

"Blake, have you heard anything from Gio?" Max asked. I couldn't bear to respond.

I pulled the covers over my head and laid there in stillness, trying to understand everything that had happened. Gio and Sam had a plan to escape, but there was no way of knowing if they'd been successful. Tomas was in custody and his brother, who seemed to be the one pulling all the strings had gone into hiding. So far, Carlos, Lola, Ricardo, and Chela were safe. My eyes filled with tears, and I just let myself cry some more.

Eventually, I got up and went back into the living room. I turned on the news channel hoping that there might be some information, but American news seldom covered what was going on in Mexico. A little while later Mia texted to see how I was feeling. I told her I was still processing and feeling pretty down.

"Any word from Gio?" she asked.

My heart lurched again. "No," I said.

I opened my laptop and searched for Tomas Barajas, there was a small article on a Mexican news site about his arrest, but there were very few details.

I made myself some toast, trying to force some calories into my depleted body and then I laid back on the sofa and pulled the blankets over me.

When I woke up again, the sun was going down. There was another message from Max asking if I'd heard anything from Gio. I replied and told him I hadn't yet. He asked to let him know if I heard anything.

Even though I knew what the end result would be, I tried calling Gio's number. It went straight to voicemail. As I heard his voice on the message, my heart hurt, and my eyes welled up with tears. I closed them and tried to breathe deeply. In my mind, I heard Gio's voice reminding me, *"As soon as I'm safe, you'll be the first to know."*

When I woke up in the morning, I had a bunch of texts from Mia.

"Call me when you're up," she had said. Then a little while later, "Are you okay?"

I picked up the phone and dialed her number. She answered right away.

"Hi!" she said. "I was worried when I didn't hear from you!"

"I'm sorry," I said. "My ringer was off, and I needed to catch up on some sleep I think."

"Have you eaten?" she asked. "Have you showered?"

"Neither," I said. "I've been pretty wiped out.

"Do you want to grab lunch?" she asked. "I feel like you should get out of the house. It's such a beautiful day."

I walked over to the windows and opened the curtains. It was in fact a beautiful day outside. "Give me an hour," I said. "I need to get ready."

"Okay, I'll come pick you up then!" she said. "And turn your ringer on please!"

"Okay, okay!" I replied. I switched it on.

I went into the bathroom and started the shower. Then I got undressed and stood under the hot water. As the warm water washed over me, I felt my shoulders relax and then I felt the rest of my body follow suit. I washed my hair, washed my body, shaved my legs... I tried to will myself into feeling normal. I got out of the shower, toweled off and went and got some clothes. I got dressed and did my make up while my hair was piled on top of my head under the towel. Eventually I combed out my hair and turned on the hairdryer.

As I started to dry my hair in sections, I thought about Gio. How I needed to just try and trust that he knew what he was doing. Max had reminded me at the airport not to panic until we knew something concrete. And didn't they always say that no news is good news? If something had happened to him, surely someone would have gotten in touch with our Mexican colleagues, and wouldn't they have called me? I wanted so badly to hear my phone ring that I could almost hear my ring tone through the sound of the hairdryer. *There you go again Blake! Getting lost in your fantasies.*

But then I heard it again, more clearly this time. I switched off the hairdryer and realized my phone was actually ringing. I could hear my phone ringing. I dropped the hairdryer on the counter and went running to my bedroom. I grabbed my phone off my nightstand just as the call ended. It was from an unknown number.

My heart kicked into overdrive.

"Oh my god, please call back!" I begged aloud. "Please call back!" My eyes filled with tears as I sat on the bed. My heart was beating out of my chest. *Was it Gio? Would he leave a message?* The tears fell down my face and I squeezed my eyes shut, feeling so much frustration and anguish.

When the phone began to ring again, I gasped aloud and nearly dropped it. It was an unknown number calling again. I took a sharp inhale as I pushed the button to answer it and my hands shook as I lifted it to my ear.

"Hello?" I answered.

There was a sigh of relief on the other end of the line, and then my heart swelled as I heard the words I'd been longing to hear for days. "Bella, I'm safe."

ABOUT THE AUTHOR

Lo Palomar is a consultant in the US and has worked around the globe on various projects. She attended Southern Methodist University in Dallas, Texas, where she received degrees in Marketing and Spanish.

Crying on Airplanes is her debut novel, and she was inspired to write the book over brunch with her best girlfriends. Laughing about what the title of their life memoirs should be called, Palomar joked that with more than 100 nights in hotels and 100,000 airline miles per year, her memoir should be called, "Crying on Airplanes." The story itself was inspired by her time working in Mexico City.

Palomar loves to travel and hopes you will enjoy exploring Mexico City through her eyes. She lives in San Diego, California and when she is not working or writing, you can catch her at the beach surfing.

Made in the USA
Las Vegas, NV
24 June 2021

25372069R00141